Also by the author

Headlock Algonquin Books

Belmondo Style St. Martin's/The Publishing Triangle's Ferro-Grumley Award

The Number of Missing Spuyten Duyvil

Both Members of the Club Texas Review Press/Clay Reynolds Prize

all around they're taking down the lights

Adam Berlin

TARTT FIRST FICTION

AWARD WINNER

Livingston Press

University of West Alabama

Library of Congress Control Number: 2024935528
Printed on acid-free paper
Printed in the United States of America by
Publishers Graphics

Typesetting and page layout: Joe Taylor, Brooke Barger
Proofreading: Kelly West, Brooke Barger

Livingston Press is part of The University of West Alabama,
and thereby has non-profit status.
Donations are tax-deductible.

6 5 4 3 2 1

all around
they're taking down the
lights

For Katherine
and our son, Eben

Stories

"Being a good actor isn't easy. Being a man is even harder.
I want to be both before I'm done."

—James Dean

hollywood but not just hollywood

Long before the drinking:

When the bathroom's empty I get the whole mirror. Bulbs instead of spotlights. Slightest eye shift magnified, Richard Gere doing low-key lines from *American Gigolo*, shift to Brando saying I could have been a contender, shift to Belmondo, he boxed too, rubbing thumb over lips, shift to Gere in *Days of Heaven*, just the look, just moving my eyes, looking away then fast at.

At the bar:

"That's what they did, drinking and smoking and driving those smooth roads and everything possible."

"Tell me some of your favorites," she says.

"They're not all great. Some of them aren't even good. And they're all way before my time. But they make me feel high, the way they look and even the way they manipulate, even when I see how manipulative they're being, I still feel it."

"Tell me some."

"*The Wild One* with Marlon Brando and *Sweet Bird of Youth* with Paul Newman and *Bullitt* with Steve McQueen and early James Bonds where the villains were characters instead of cartoons and there was more dialogue than special effects, when Sean Connery was Bond and not those others, or lesser known movies with Richard Burton when he was young or George Peppard, those movies when color was

Technicolor, and some foreign movies, the ones with that old Hollywood feel even if they weren't shot in Hollywood, movies with Oliver Reed and Jean-Paul Belmondo."

"I know most of the names, but I never saw those movies. We'll have to go sometime."

"We can go drinking and driving and watch a bunch of movies."

"And you can pretend you're high."

"It's not pretend."

After the second round:

"Like and movie. I can't see the first word."

After the fourth (maybe fifth):

"What do you do?" she says.

"I run."

"I'm a runner. That's more than running."

"I do push-ups and pull-ups."

"Very disciplined."

"When I have to be."

"What are you, a military brat?"

"Are you?"

"I'm a professor brat," she says, "which is close to a military brat. My dad traveled all over for work. We moved so much I got tired of making new friends and then leaving them, which is why I started running. Instead of playing in whatever neighborhood with whatever new kids there were, I relied on myself and ran. Now I teach that idea when we read *The Loneliness of the Long Distance Runner*. I teach and I help out with the cross-country team during the season."

"I saw the movie. Tom Courtenay. He had a good look. He

looked like a smart delinquent, not a Hollywood delinquent."

"Do you look like a delinquent when you run?"

"Probably. A real one. I don't love running, but I do it."

"You don't get a runner's high?"

"I don't."

"That's too bad."

I raise my glass.

"I get a three-count high when I ask the bartender to tip the bottle and pour heavy. And then in the morning I run, even when I'm hung over."

"Your penance," she says.

"My penance. I absolve myself and do it all over again."

I down my drink.

"Another?"

"You're fast," she says.

"Fast. Where are you staying?"

"A cheapy hotel called the Belnord."

"Near here."

"Near here. You are fast."

I rub my thumb across my lips like Belmondo.

"Do you know that movie?"

"I do," she says. "He looks like a Hollywood delinquent."

"He was a tough guy first. And he was playing Hollywood, so he looked Hollywood, but not today-Hollywood."

"I believe you."

"It's a great movie. It's like life should be."

"Let's leave the car stealing and the cop shooting for the movies," she says.

"Let's hold onto the thumb across the lips."

"We can do that."

We leave the bar and walk to her hotel. It's between avenues and from outside looks like a regular apartment building. The lobby has two over-stuffed chairs facing each other, a small desk, and a man standing behind the desk reading a book.

The elevator's built for one and a half people.

The bed's most of the room.

Bags on the floor, Soho stores, Fifth Avenue stores, one from Nike that's full.

"You've been shopping."

"I went to some museums first."

"Penance. You're off the hook. Running shoes?"

"Nike Frees. They feel like nothing at all."

After smoking in the hotel:

One song from her phone into the next into the next and traffic noise and sleep breathing and car lights moving along ceiling and room sliding away and one time running I hit a hole, fell, hit my head, and I was in a field with long, swaying grasses that would be browner in reality but all green, bright green, infused green, Technicolor-movie green, and the bluest sky, no clouds anywhere, and the sun was somehow behind the blue, invisible but lighting the sky, and I was looking up at this bluest blue and seeing myself at the same time lying in the greenest green and I wanted to be there, surrounded by bright and warm and color and then I was back on the city sidewalk. I stood and knew I'd been knocked out. I wanted to go back there, at least for a while, back to the place where the sun was behind the sky lighting, brighting everything.

After dreaming of driving:

"You kept saying you look like you," she says.

Steve McQueen in *Bullitt.*

Ryan O'Neal in *The Driver*.

Alain Delon in *Le Samourai*.

Whoever's playing Bond in every James Bond movie.

They say I look like Daniel Craig in the first one.

They say I look like Richard Gere when he started.

"Do you look like you?" she says.

After:

The last scene's the best when it's happening if the movie's good enough, real-life good but not so real-life not enough happens. The walk-out song with credits rolling almost as right-there as coming attractions, those compilations of first moments all in a row when the lights aren't all the way down but inspiring in the easiest Hollywood way, fake inspiring if you're not blurring your eyes or if you're not sitting back and letting the screen hit you and it doesn't even matter that the lights aren't all the way down, one preview jumping to the next, accelerated moments, different characters in different places in different relationships and the best lines pulled and delivered without context, visual anarchy that could lead to uprisings if everyone wasn't just sitting and watching and taking in, and the music and the movement and the light, higher than life, possibility of everything, and the movie begins, the one we're all waiting for, all of us in this wide dark room with all the build-up inside all of us together, united and waiting and hopeful, and the lights go all the way down until it's all-dark except for neon-red EXIT signs making that dark more exciting, more expectant, and the music starts and the opening credits and things start happening, unexpected things, pretend but not just pretend, Hollywood but not just Hollywood, and it isn't even the movie but the beginning the beginning the beginning, holy, and everything possible.

makeit

Light. Sulfur. I was out of sleep. A lit match in my face and Curt sitting on my bed. Grinning. Flipping open his wallet one-handed to let me see. There they were. Fresh hundred-dollar bills in a thick stack almost sticking together.

"I couldn't lose," he said.

"What are you doing here?"

"Blackjack. A little craps. I hit on blackjack."

"Where?"

"Caesars. Look at that. Three grand. I'm telling you. I couldn't lose."

"What the fuck are you doing here?" I said.

He'd won and quit by ten. Drove his piece-of-shit Chevy Celebrity, electrician's tape holding together the windshield, all the way from Atlantic City to see me, and in great time, under five hours speeding on the turnpikes. Curt lit another match. My phone showed 2:48. Curt's face was all shadows, but his grin was clear.

"You jerk off tonight? You turn around and face the wall, so he won't see you? You like having a guy sleeping five feet across from you?"

"It's the way they set these dorm rooms up."

"What the fuck are you doing here?" he said.

"That's the real question," he said.

He was looking around in the dark. At the small fridge. At

the wall above my roommate's bed. I had posters like that when I was twelve. Girls with big tits and hair, small swimsuits. My roommate, pretending sleep on the other side of the room, was doing a shit job. Too stiff. Too quiet. I hated him. His name was Mark. He went to bed at 11 every night. He set his alarm, bird chirps, for 6 every morning. He made straining sounds when he bent to tie his shoes. He put acne medicine on his forehead that stunk the place up. He constantly turned from his anally-arranged desk, desk lamp exaggerating his split ends, to ask me questions, mostly about how I got so many girls. His words. Got so many girls. I told him I'd treat him to a hooker on his nineteenth birthday if he didn't get his first fuck by then. He'd giggle and wipe his nose, all that excitement making his snot run.

Curt was lighting another match.

I rubbed my hands over my face to wake up. I was beat. I had a 10 o'clock *Intro to Theater*. I'd stayed too late at the campus bar, first beers, then shots when I started talking to a pretty sophomore, trying to feel some connection, hoping the alcohol would make me feel like I cared. Curt smiled, softer now, glad to see me, the shadow of a dimple in his left cheek. My head hurt.

"I can't believe you found me."

"I came to visit," Curt said. "Look at that."

He riffled the bills, but I couldn't see them anymore. The match was out. The bills sounded crisp, sounded like a lot of money for Curt and me.

"Let's get out of here," I said.

I put on jeans, sneakers, and a T I'd worn only once, new for college. My roommate didn't move. I knew he was forcing his eyes closed, keeping his body still, holding his breath. My eyes were adjusting, and I could see his shoes set neatly at attention in front of his bed. I could smell his fucking acne medicine on his greasy forehead. I shut the door hard behind us.

Fluorescent lights. Blue-tiled hall. Garbage on the floor. Empty cups. Beer cans. Hip-hop beats coming from a room down the hall. Someone had stapled a James Dean poster to the bathroom door, *Every 1's A Rebel* written in pen across the bottom. Curt looked at me. He knew he didn't have to say anything. He ripped the poster off the door and threw it in the trash can outside the bathroom. I didn't care. I was about ready to quit. The other guys in the hall were kids. Sometimes when they were trying to hook up, when they had her in the room but not between the sheets, they'd blast their music, like the bass beats mirrored the size of their cocks. I knew what they were doing. Talking and talking and not making a move. Sometimes I was trying to sleep, tired from running twice around campus to sweat out the grease from my Financial Aid job flipping burgers. Sometimes when it was too late and their music too loud, I'd take off my clothes and walk down the hall nice and slow with my cock hanging porno-smooth under the fluorescents, and open their doors and walk into their rooms, say to those college boys trying to impress, You should turn the music down, delivered low-key, not enunciating any one word. The college boys jumped. Better than if I threatened them. Better than if I kicked in their speakers. I always stood there until the girl looked at my cock. The boys couldn't hold my eyes for shit.

"Let's get a drink," Curt said.

"There's nothing open around here. Not now."

"Any girls around?"

"It's too late. We can go down to the lounge and see if anyone passes through. You can buy me a soda."

"I can buy you a hundred sodas," Curt said, tapping his right front pocket where he kept his wallet.

We walked down the hall. Curt looked around, shook his head

like *What the fuck are you doing here when we were having so much fun?*

"You doing well in school? You like it? You like being in college?"

"It's okay."

"You got to get back to the city."

"And do what?"

"Do what we did," he said.

We'd met in the city. Both too young to be living on our own. Fucking around on the streets. Going out every night.

We'd met in acting class, got kicked out two weeks later for laughing while two bad actors did an improv about love gone wrong.

Our teacher's name was Rochelle. She had bad hair and wore black jeans so tight you could see her camel toe. For one exercise, she made us pretend to take showers. To feel the water. To smell the soap. To hear our feet against wet linoleum. She was full of sensory shit. She hadn't been in anything we'd ever seen, so it didn't matter when she told us to leave her class. I told her to fuck herself and Curt followed me down the stairs, leaving the wannabes behind.

So we spent the days walking Manhattan doing our own acting exercises.

We wandered the department stores, talked in fake languages to the women who worked the perfume counters, making them understand with hand gestures how we were looking to buy expensive fragrances for our girlfriends in Norway or Denmark or whatever blond nation they thought we were from. They'd name countries and languages, hoping to pinpoint us, hoping for a nod of recognition, while we spoke nonsense and shook our blond heads in diagonals. When the item was finally agreed upon, our hands covered with a dozen sweet smells, and they put the chosen bottle of perfume on the counter, one of us would take a nickel from our pocket and put it on the counter like that would cover the cost. When they said No, that's not enough, we pretended to understand, took back the nickel, and shelled out two or three pennies. Soon management was out of the woodwork trying to explain American money to us. Eventually we'd thank the salespeople in perfect English and walk out of the store.

We staged fights in the street, brutal and real looking. Whole crowds gathered, watching us beat each other, until we both stood and took our bows. One time a cop took Curt down, nightstick against neck, and I had to explain we were just fucking around. I told the cop it was for an acting class, an exercise. He told us to do our exercises somewhere else.

We impersonated police officers around the TKTS line where tourists waited for half-price Broadway shows. Acted official, warning out-of-towners to keep moving single file, no talking allowed. When they asked who we were we told them Undercover officers, which shut them up and kept them walking single file and silent. One time we told an undercover officer to keep moving. He and his partner put the cuffs on, started walking us to the precinct. The real cop was easy to read, trying to scare us, so we acted scared. He let us go.

Curt had spent two years in a juvenile detention center. I'd left home a day after high school graduation after smashing my parents' Volvo. I was speeding through an intersection and a guy hit me and I got out of the car and went after him. It was my fault, but I didn't care. I'd been planning on leaving for New York anyway. And then I met Curt. We were paired up in acting class. We both liked old movies. We both did Marlon Brando's voice, both recited his speech, *I coulda been a contender*.

Most nights ended in the cheap pussy places around Times Square. We went into booths, never too close to each other, fed tokens, and watched the dancers shake their asses. For ten bucks they'd let customers finger them. One time we saw a guy eating out one of the girls and we heard each other laughing, which made us laugh more. We kept feeding tokens to see how deep the guy could get his tongue in.

"What do you want?"

"Grape," I said.

The dorm lounge was empty. Curt slipped in two bucks and got two sodas. We touched cans.

"To three-thousand dollars," I said. "Good job."

"It was easy. I got eleven blackjacks. Eleven. I counted."

"We never had luck like that."

"We can live on this for a month. We can eat at decent places, go to some clubs, get some new clothes."

"White sneakers."

"All white. None of that gray shit."

We bought gray sneakers so they wouldn't look dirty too quickly. Living low. Curt bussed tables at an Italian place downtown. I ran lunches up and down 47th Street, the Diamond District, just east of the Broadway theaters. Taking tips from bridge-and-tunnel secretaries and salesmen with manicured hands, big diamonds on their fingers with bigger diamonds under the glass cases in front of them, price tags filled with zeros. The big shots would hand me a buck. *Boy.* That's how they looked at me. *Here, boy.*

"We'll start fucking around again," Curt said. "You know you miss it."

"I don't know."

I drank some grape soda. It was too sweet.

"You like it here?" he said.

"I don't know."

"What do you do? You go to class every day?"

"It's not high school. Classes meet a couple times a week."

"What else?"

"I have a Financial Aid job."

"Doing what?"

"I work in the dining hall."

"Doing what?"

"I flip burgers."

"You can flip burgers in the city. I bet we can find you a job flipping burgers, no problem." Curt's dimple was out.

"I study some. I've fucked a couple of coeds."

"You fucked college girls in New York. How far's the center of Boston?"

"Not far."

"We can drive in and fuck around. Something's got to be open."

"It's not like New York."

"I could have told you that. Where's the skyline? Where's all the people? You know you miss it."

"I miss some of it."

"Then come back. We'll have a great time. We were having a great time. You don't belong here."

The lounge was bright. Bright light. Bright orange couches. Bright rust-colored carpet. A color scheme to scare off lurking intruders. There had been two on-campus rapes the year before, that's what the dorm counselor said, night one, all the entering freshmen sitting around in a circle like at a fucking campfire, flames blazing, marshmallows to roast. The dorm counselor talked about room maintenance, the college's policy on lost IDs, the rules about quiet hours. I wanted to ask if he'd change my diaper but kept quiet.

Curt looked good. He'd been out in the sun, he said. Lying on a towel in Washington Square. Doing bar dips on the jungle gym in the kid park off Minetta since they'd removed the parallel bars where we'd worked out. It wasn't even October. I hadn't even been away a month. Curt tipped his soda, gulped it down like it was the world's best drink. The can covered the scar between his nose and upper lip. He did everything cool. A beefy James Dean. I was a Richard Gere type. We liked the old-school actors. Even last week a couple holding hands whispered I looked like a blond Richard Gere, like he looked in *An Officer and a Gentleman*. They were watching me, me fucking around the streets of Boston that closed too early, acting crazed, jumping and shaking and screaming in tongues, not the same though, not the same without Curt there, my audience, or me his audience, fucking around together, not alone.

"How'd you find this place?" I said.

"I asked directions once I got close. Some drunk kids showed me where the students lived. They were the only ones out."

"What else is going on in New York?"

"I went to a couple auditions from *Backstage*."

"Anything good?"

"A low-budget movie. The assistant checked me out in the waiting room. I bet they'll call."

"What movie?"

"I don't know. They hadn't come up with an official title yet. I saw Pacino walking on Madison Avenue. He's a fucking midget. He's an old fucking man."

"Like DeNiro."

"Fucking DeNiro. What a pussy. All those tough guy roles and he still ducked out."

"He's an actor," I said.

"*You looking at me?*"

"He's also old."

We'd followed him one night for five blocks and he kept peeking over his shoulder until he ducked into a doorman building. We'd been thinking we'd kick his ass and make the news, get some publicity. We had all sorts of schemes.

"Come back," Curt said. "It's only a matter of time before we make it."

That was the word.

"Come on," Curt said.

"I've got to finish the semester at least."

"No you don't. You hate it here."

"Everyone hates it at the beginning."

"I'm telling you. We got what it takes. We got all the moves. We do shit no one else does. We'll make it."

The word. Two words really but said so often it became one. Makeit. Going to Makeit. Got what it takes to Makeit.

I didn't say anything.

"You auditioning here? Is there stuff to audition for?"

"I got a small part in a production."

"What kind of part?"

"I play a soldier. In a Plautus play. *The Braggart Soldier*."

"A Plautus play? What the fuck is that?"

"It's some Roman comedy."

"That will get you far."

"It's good practice."

"You're not cut out for stage. We got to do films. All that fucking around prepared us. You can't do that on stage."

"You do a part on stage, a real part, you'll have no problem in front of the camera. That's why we went to New York."

"That's not why. They're always yelling on stage. It's not real. There's nothing real about it. It's nothing like film. New York's where the real casting takes place. That's why I came to New York. It's where Brando started and DeNiro and James Dean, all of them. They all got their breaks in New York. It's where Richard Gere started."

"He didn't."

"He was in New York. They did stage work to break in, but they all wanted to be movie stars. What the fuck? Where is everybody? Aren't there any females at this college?"

"It's three in the morning."

"What's up with all the lights in this room? It's like a prison. What do you do all day?"

"I don't know."

I walked over to the TV and turned it on. A repeat of *The Love Boat*. We sat on the orange couches and watched for a while. Curt lit up a cigarette and threw the pack at me. I hadn't smoked all month. The guy playing the captain was speaking in double-entendres about a couple in the honeymoon suite. I took a cigarette and Curt lit me. The laugh track kept coming up.

"Would you say he made it?" I said.

"The captain guy? He probably made some money, but he didn't make it. We're talking about him, but he didn't make it like we're going to make it. I don't know his name. It's TV. We're cut out for film."

A girl walked into the lounge. She had a book with her. A novel, not a text. Her hand covered the title. She wore a tank top. No bra. Big tits. Curt put out his cigarette in the can and pressed the can with his thumbs to make that aluminum popping sound. He had three grand in his wallet. He still thought he was going to make it. My head hurt. I'd started with beers. I'd ordered my first shot when the sophomore asked my major. I'd ordered my second shot when she told me about her internship plans. The girl in the tank top smiled at Curt.

"Long night at the library?" Curt said.

Like he'd always been here. Like he'd seen the line in a script about college life and rehearsed it to perfection, practiced it over and over in the long bathroom mirror while his roommate applied zit medicine to his forehead a couple sinks down. Like the close-up was his, and he knew just how to move his eyes, his lips, flare his nostrils so even his scar looked good. He had it down and I'd had it down, knew how to look just right for the camera, we'd filmed each other with our phones, but there were no cameras when I delivered lunches up and down 47th Street, no close-ups when I counted tips at the end of my shift.

"I was just taking a walk," she said. The too-bright light showed too-thin lips, a pushed-in nose.

"It's a nice night for walking," Curt said.

"I haven't seen you around here before," she said.

"Have you seen him?" Curt glanced at me.

"I haven't seen either of you," she said.

"We keep a low profile except at night. Then we're all over the place. You want to hang out? You want a soda?"

"Sure."

He got up and smiled his dimpled smile and went over to the soda machine with his bulging wallet out.

"What kind?"

"Diet Coke. Thanks."

Curt slipped in the bill and the soda came down. *The Love Boat* music came on and then the commercial.

"You're cute," he said.

She wasn't, but she was the only girl around. We'd done shit. He'd done shit. More shit than me. We'd fucked around on Manhattan's streets, but now we were in a college lounge. Curt handed her the soda.

I took the last hit off my cigarette.

I listened to him move the conversation to sex. First he joked about why she was out. Then he asked if she was visiting her boyfriend. When she refused to tell us he pressed her, smiling, flirting, until she admitted she had no boyfriend, that she slept late and studied late, that she took walks around campus at night hoping she'd meet someone.

"Someone special?" Curt asked.

"Maybe," she said.

"You can tell us."

"I said maybe."

"I like the way you smile," he said.

She was eating it up. She'd never had so much attention. I watched Curt work. I watched the girl. *The Love Boat* came back on.

"Let's go back there," Curt said.

There was a small room off the lounge. The door was open. Extra orange chairs stacked on each other and half a ping-pong table propped against the wall.

"Why?" she said.

"It's more private. Come on, it will be fun. We're two good-looking guys. You know it."

"You are."

"We're going to make it soon. We have some big things in the works."

"Like what?"

"You don't recognize us?"

"No."

"We've done soap work. We have a movie project lined up. We're here to take theater classes, work on technique."

"You're not full-time students?"

"We're not even part-time. The producers sent us here to

study."

"I hear it's a good theater department," she said.

"It is. Come on. Let's go in there. It's more private."

Curt kept his eyes on her eyes. She flushed. She probably hadn't even been kissed in a long time. There was no one around.

"All right," she said.

People fell for shit all the time. We snuck into the Equity Lounge without union cards, told the monitor at the door I'd cut my hand, could we please just use their bathroom and wash up. A ketch-up-soaked napkin wrapped around my fingers did the trick. Once inside, we stormed an audition room and started doing a song-and-dance routine for two men and two women behind a desk, laptops open, headshots on their screens. We gyrated around the hardwood floor. We belted out *Getting to Know You*. One of the men walked out of the room and soon security was kicking us out but not before we told everyone to look at us, screaming we were going to make it, screaming we had the balls to make it.

We went into the small room. Curt closed the door and pushed the broken ping-pong table against it. I sat on one of the orange chairs and watched him make out with her. He put his hand under her shirt and started to squeeze her tits. He tried getting his hand in her pants. She wouldn't let him. Come on, he said. She let him rub her cunt from the outside. He took off her tank top. Her tits were full, her nipples long and pink. He played with her nipples and asked if she wanted me to play with them and she said Sure. He walked her over to me and I took one tit and he took the other and he laughed. Curt said we could fuck her and no one would know. She moved away from our hands. She tried to move away. Curt stood in front of her. He asked if she wanted to suck our cocks. She looked at the floor. He laughed and said he was only joking. She put her shirt back on. I moved the ping-pong table away from the door.

"We're going to make it," he said.

She left the room with her shirt untucked and her hair messed up. She'd forgotten to take her book. Curt threw it in the garbage.

"What a pig," Curt said.

I didn't say anything.

"What's the problem? She agreed to everything. She can tell everyone she fooled around with two guys at once."

"You scared her."

"She wasn't scared. She knew I wasn't going to do anything."

"She was scared."

"What if she was? We can use that. We'll be able to use that one day. There's always a scene where someone's scared. I bet you haven't done anything like that since you left New York. You got to come back."

"We weren't getting anywhere."

"We didn't put in enough time. We were just starting. I got three grand. We'll go to auditions. We'll drop by every casting agency. We'll send our headshots everywhere."

"I erased my headshots."

"Why'd you do that?"

"I don't need them here."

"We'll get you new ones. That's easy. Come on. We can pack up your shit in a minute. If we leave now, we'll be back in the city before the 9 o'clock rush."

"I've got class tomorrow."

"Fuck the class," Curt said. "I was walking around two nights ago and they were shooting on the street. I didn't even recognize the actor, but there was a whole crowd around watching him like he was the man. All the lights were set up. They had two cameras, one on ground level and another on one of those beams to get a high-angle shot. I was right there. It was just a matter of stepping into that light. A few feet away and I could have been the star. We're that close. We're that fucking close. All we got to do is walk those few feet into the light and we're in, we're in, and once we get our break we'll make it. We're more interesting than any one of them. We've done more shit than any of them. We know how to fuck around and everything we've done will come off on film."

"We're not that close."

"We are if we try. I'm telling you. I was just a few feet away from those lights."

I'd done my own practicing. Did it here even. Couldn't help myself sometimes. When the bathroom was empty and I had the whole long mirror to myself, fluorescents my spotlights. The smallest gesture magnified, the slightest shift of my eye. I'd heard the stories of lucky breaks. Of getting discovered. I'd also seen the numbers. Lines of actors at cattle calls. Packed waiting rooms for bullshit auditions. And here wasn't better. I wasn't enjoying my acting class. I wasn't enjoying rehearsals for my walk-on. I hated holding that spear. We could fuck around on three grand for a couple weeks and then I'd need a job. Curt had more faith than me. He'd been dreaming Hollywood for longer, he'd been more down and out, so maybe he'd had more need to dream. Dreams of making it. Dreams of making it all the way. I'd see the girl in the library and she'd look at me and I'd look at her and I'd do my take, put all the meaning of everything we'd done in that one glance, that one small narrowing of my eyes, but she'd be the only one to see, and she'd move her eyes and keep them away like she'd kept them away before I moved the ping-pong table and she left the small room, left the student lounge, and even if I told her he wasn't me, even if I told her about New York and acting class and making it, even if I told her that was our bond, had been our bond, making it more important than everything else, fuck it to everything else, no fucking rules, anarchy making the best actors, and how it wasn't my everything anymore and without the everything I'd never make it the way I'd dreamed of making it, it wasn't even a dream anymore, not really, not enough, she'd still keep her eyes away from everything in my eyes while students walked by carrying books to check out.

"Well?" Curt said.

"You want to spend the night? You tired?"

"Not me. I'm wired. I'm ready to go."

Curt looked around the lounge. He took out his pack of cigarettes, took one out, lit up. He inhaled slow, exhaled cool.

"Come with me," he said.

"I can't."

"You don't belong in this place. You think these other students are barricading women in storage rooms and feeling their tits while they tell you how good-looking you are? You think these other students know what's out there? You want to go back to that dorm room and get into bed five feet away from that fucker you probably can't stand? You know you're good."

"I don't know."

"We're good. We're more than good. We're going to make it."

The last prank we played before I left, our last day of fucking around, we were walking near Rockefeller Center. There had been a couple of mounted police looking over the crowd and when they rode away there was a load of horse shit on the street. I took a napkin from a hot dog vendor and picked up the most perfectly round piece of shit I could find. We walked into Teuscher Chocolates. The place was packed. Beautiful arrangements of expensive Swiss chocolates filled the counters and tables. Curt asked the saleswoman a question to make sure her back stayed turned. I placed the round piece of horse shit at the center of a display of champagne truffles. I walked over to Curt. We looked at the display. We started laughing, uncontrollable laughing, the kind of laughing that took our breath away. The saleswoman was looking at us. We couldn't move we were laughing so hard. It was too ridiculous seeing that piece of horse shit pretending it was a truffle. We finally left the store. We walked around for a while, fucked with some tourists, staged a final fight. When we walked by Teuscher Chocolates a half hour later there was no one inside but the help. They were searching through all the candy looking for shit.

practice makes

I was squeezing. She was watching.

Even in camp, even when I was around all those boys all the time, like kids in the same family, and there had been two stalls just for our bunk, and doors on the stalls I could lock, I'd wake before anyone, before the counselors even, walk across the cold floorboards, open the door, close the door, sit. And the rest of my life, in college, traveling, at work, it was the same. If I couldn't shit in peace, I wouldn't shit at all. Soon I wasn't going to have any peace. Not for three years. I didn't know what kind of food they'd serve inside. I didn't know what the routine would be. I didn't know if most inmates shit in the morning or the evening. What I did know was there were no doors on the stalls and I'd be shitting in front of men. Like a runner before a multi-year marathon, I decided to get in shape, to bank the miles in my legs, to practice, so when race day came I'd be ready. Race day was in one week.

With one week left, I told the woman I was seeing, a new woman, a woman I'd met after I'd pleaded and was sentenced, what I needed from her. Her name was Wendi. She'd been cool from the first second. I put everything in terms of time these days, and in the smallest fraction of time she took me in, even when I told her my story. I'd been wall-punching drunk that night. My knuckles were already skinned and bleeding when I saw her at the bar looking at me. She had smart eyes, the kind of eyes I liked. They didn't have to be baby blue or exotic green. She had clear, smart eyes and great eyebrows that framed her smart eyes, and so, drunk, always big-balled when drunk, big enough to get me three years, I walked over to her. I didn't say anything. I just walked over and nodded my head and she kept her smart eyes on my drunk eyes. Women never knew how drunk I was, I could talk sober until I drank the drink that put me down, but Wendi knew I was fucked-up. From the first second she knew. But she stood there, calm, with this drunk in front of her, me, just standing there too, not feeding her any shit, not even talking.

"Is that the best you've got?" she said and looked serious for one second, two seconds, three seconds, and smiled. She had an up-to-something smile but sweet too, like her mischief would never go mean or hurtful.

"It is the best I've got," I said.

"No clever openings?"

"No lines for me. Not those kinds of lines. Take me or leave me. Or just look at me. You have smart eyes."

"Smart eyes," she said. "I've never heard that one."

"I'm an original," I said. "Like a fucking Van Gogh. I'm drinking tonight until everything gets all swirly. Why don't you join me?"

"Will you give me your ear?"

"Tonight I will."

"And tomorrow?"

"Tomorrow I'll be sober and you won't want my ear."

"Are you no fun when you're not drunk?"

"I'm a lot of fun."

"What if I still want your ear?"

"Wake up with me tomorrow and we'll see how it goes."

"I'm drinking Jameson," she said and smiled her smile.

I ordered two shots of Jameson, two bottles of Bud, we touched glasses, held each other's eyes like we were supposed to when toasting something important.

"To now," I said.

She shot her whiskey like a pro. I waited for her eyes to narrow, her lips to purse, the slightest sign of burn, but she just kept her eyes on mine.

"So what's your story?" I said.

"No story. We're drinking to now, remember?"

"Let's have another shot. We can drink to yesterday."

"Get me another shot and maybe I'll tell you a story," she said.

I ordered two more shots. We touched to yesterday, downed them. I concentrated on keeping my eyes and mouth as steady as hers. Mind over matter. I'd been thinking about mind over matter a lot lately. I stood in my closet for a full hour every afternoon since I'd been sentenced, stood still, just held myself in that small space, practicing for life in a cell. I forced myself to take it. When I opened the door, the extra air smelled like freedom.

"So what's your story?" she said almost like I'd said it.

I was drunk. My drunk could go two ways. I could go happy, like the world was beautiful. When I went happy, I laughed a lot and smiled a lot and fell in fake love, fast. Or I could go angry. I hadn't figured out how many seconds went into three years, a little less for good behavior. Good behavior. I would try to be good. I would try to keep to myself. I would try to block everything out, so much blocking I'd be able to shit in an open stall as easily as a private room. When I came up for parole, they'd see I was a model inmate and set me free to breathe free air. But I'd be a different man when I walked out. I already knew that. I already knew I'd be able to do some real damage when I was done, which was stupid thinking but what I thought, drunk and sober.

"I'm not interested in my story," I said.

"Is it a boring story?"

"It is to me."

"I like your hands," she said and smiled. "The blood really brings out your skin tones."

"Wall punching," I said. "If you loved me, would you wash my hands?"

"I do love you," she said.

I smiled. I lifted my hands in front of my face. Three knuckles, the same three knuckles on each hand, were bloody. I had very red blood. I usually hated the sight of it, but when I was drunk blood worked like a red badge, made me feel tough. When I was drunk, I wasn't so scared about going in. When I was sober, every prison movie haunted me. I knew what I should do. I should walk through the gate, look the hardest fucker in the face, wait for him to say something, throw the first punch. But that would add time and I was more scared of time. Time was bigger, badder, stronger than any man.

"Then clean me up. Clean up my hands."

"Tell me your story about wall punching," she said. "How come you're so angry?"

"I'm just angry."

"I'm Wendi," she said.

"You tell me your story, Wendi. I bought you drinks. The least you can do is tell me your story."

"Fair is fair," she said, but she just stood there.

"I think you drank enough," she said.

"Maybe. Maybe not."

Wendi leaned over the bar. The bartender came right to her. She was the kind of woman who got served right away and I was with her and the world looked beautiful and I was free. Right now, I was free. A month seemed a long way away. Three years seemed so long I couldn't do it.

We touched shots. The Jameson went straight to my head. I held onto the bar and the dizziness passed.

"My drink. Your story," she said, and her smart eyes stayed on mine, taking me in, ready for whatever I had to say. "Tell me."

I told her my story. I told her how I went out drinking one night, too much drinking, and a bartender cut me off. I was standing next to two women, not talking yet, just drinking, and the bartender told them they were safe with him, like I was some lecherous fuck who didn't know how to pick up women. Picking up women was the best thing I did. I could pick up any woman, beyond lines, beyond lechery, and here was this man playing protector, thinking his position behind the bar made his balls bigger than my balls. I called him on it. I told him I was a bartender. I told him standing behind a bar didn't mean much. He had nothing to say, no easy comeback. I called him on it again, told him to show me how tough he was. He cut me off. I finished my drink, the slowest drink I ever drank. I went to another bar. I replayed the scene, too many times. The way it happened. The way I wished it had happened, those coulda-shoulda scenarios everyone plays too late. I didn't want it to be too late. I walked back to the bar, waited across the street, waited and waited, and finally the lights went out and the bartender came out, kissed one of the waitresses good-night, and started walking alone. I followed him until there was no one around, which wasn't easy, there was always someone around in Manhattan, and I touched his shoulder and asked if he could protect himself, forget the women, if he could protect himself outside the fucking bar. His eyes went scared and I hit him. He went down. It wasn't out of me. I was angry drunk. I was kicking him. That's what the cops wrote in their report. They turned the corner in their cruiser and saw a White male dressed in jeans and a white T kicking another man on the ground. My lawyer said I shouldn't bother with a trial. I pleaded out to three years.

It seemed a lot, but the bartender was in the hospital for a week. He'd suffered a concussion and one of his broken ribs had punctured his lung. That was my story.

"Did you do any time?" Wendi said. She hadn't flinched once.

"Not yet. I go in, in a month. Twenty-six days, actually. I go upstate in twenty-six days. A place called Bare Hill. It sounds like camp."

"How will you spend your last days out?"

"Packing every minute with a good time. Care to join me?"

"Of course," she said. "It's perfect. Twenty-six days is the exact number of days it takes for me to get sick of someone. At the very moment I start tiring of you, you'll be gone."

"Like magic," I said.

"Like that," she said and snapped her fingers in front of my face.

"I'm drunk," I said.

"Come," she said and took my forearm in her hand. "I'll take you home. I'll clean up your hands. We'll fall in love for twenty-six days and then we'll say goodbye."

In the morning, my knuckles stung. Without alcohol to cool the nerve endings, every time my knuckles slid across her sheets it hurt. I kept my eyes from showing pain and kept moving inside her. She was fun in bed. Serious when she came. Playful after she came. Whenever we took a break, I took her hand and placed it on my cock and she just kept her hand there, moving her fingers slowly, putting me to sleep.

I spent that morning with her. And the next morning. And the next. She worked as a designer for a tie company, her fingers moving over different fabrics, her eyes surveying different patterns, predicting the next big trend. I'd quit my job at the restaurant. They would have fired me anyway and I wanted some time off before I had a different kind of time off. We spent twenty-one nights together, woke up twenty-one mornings. I had five days left.

I was squeezing. She was watching.

"I can't," I said.

"You will."

"I can't."

"You'll have to so you will."

"I'll explode in there."

"No. You will. You will here. You will in front of me. And you will there. I have faith."

"This isn't related to faith," I said.

"It is," Wendi said.

"I can't right now. I'll try again tomorrow."

"You look sexy even on the pot," she said.

I rested my head on my fist like *The Thinker*.

"I always thought he was doing that too," she said.

I took my head off my fist. My knuckles were all healed. I hadn't felt like punching a wall since I'd met Wendi.

"I can cook tonight if you want. Or we can go out. Whatever you want."

"What do you want?" I said.

I wasn't squeezing anymore so it was just me sitting there, my cock hanging between my legs, no big deal, no more pressure. I'd try again tomorrow morning. Her eyes were still the smartest eyes I'd ever seen and every morning, every morning, I wanted her almost as much as I'd wanted her the night before. I'd always been a hit-and-run man, but with her I had no desire to run. Even in the afternoons, before she came home from work, when I went to some happy-hour bar and had a few drinks and watched the women, I had no desire to flirt. Maybe it was the twenty-six-day thing. Time was running out and what we had would just end. The end was part of our beginning. No pressure.

"I'll cook," she said.

"I could eat your linguine with pesto every day."

"We had that two days ago."

"I'll dream about your pesto."

"I'll pick up some basil on the way home," she said. She was still sitting on the bathmat, watching me.

She stood. I stood. There was nothing there. I flushed the toilet anyway.

I walked into her living room and turned on the TV. Tourists pressed against the barriers at Rockefeller Center, unpaid extras for *Today.* B-level models walked a makeshift runway showing off wedding gowns while the lucky couple who'd get married in Barbados, compliments of the show, looked on, their stupid, smiling faces caught in close-up after each model turned and walked away.

The shower went on. The shower went off. Wendi kissed me goodbye and left for work. I went straight to the bathroom and took a shit.

Wendi lived in Chelsea and worked in midtown. I'd broken my lease, sold my furniture, put my books on the street for any interested passerby, and drank everywhere. For a month, I'd done everything I wouldn't be able to do in prison. I walked through Central Park and breathed fresh air. I went to museums and movies and off-Broadway shows. I ate good food, Italian and Thai and sushi and steaks at the Strip House and seafood at Mary's Fish Camp and paella at Rio Mar and shrimp in green sauce at Sevilla. And I drank.

Time Out had written up a new bar called Amuse that had a great happy hour, cheap beers and dollar oysters. Since I was living no-time-like-the-present days and since there would be no oysters in prison, I took the subway downtown. It was just after five, it was fall, and the sky was a cold shade of blue, but inside the bar looked warm and long and there were already people filling the room, happy people with alcohol glows and easy smiles. I thought of where I'd be in five days, ordered one martini and a second and a third and like only alcohol could do, no metaphor in the world to describe that 80-proof trick that melted edges, I wasn't scared anymore. There was a fat man on my left, trying to engage two women in conversation. There was a couple on my right, asking each other first-date questions. There was a pretty bartender in front of me filling two tall glasses with beer. I put a toothpick into a cured olive and ate it, savoring the salt. When the bartender looked up, I ordered a dozen oysters.

I loved sitting in bars. Everything always seemed far away in a good way. Even my countdown of days didn't feel so urgent when I was in a bar. Sometimes I'd look at my watch, drink, look at my watch and enjoy how slow the minute was passing, like the second hand had gotten drunk and wasn't moving the way it usually did. In prison, I'd have to find the trick to speed things up. If I could do half my time, I knew the second half would go faster. I was old enough to know that much about time.

The bartender put the plate of oysters in front of me. I squeezed lemon, added horseradish and hot sauce, took the first one in my mouth. I tasted the sea and went far away.

The fat man turned. I'd only seen the width of his back and fleshy neck. His face was pig-like, eyes squinty from puffed cheeks. He was too pale. His heart, struggling all the time, had to be tired.

"How are the oysters here?"

"I haven't had oysters in a while. They taste good to me."

"They look good."

"Have one if you like."

"Really?"

"I'm feeling generous."

"Don't mind if I do," he said.

I prepared one for him, squeezed lemon, added horseradish and hot sauce. He took the oyster in his thick fingers, placed the shell in his mouth, and sucked the meat with joy.

"So how are the oysters here?" I said.

"Not bad," he said. "Not bad at all. I eat oysters everywhere. From Apalachicola on the Gulf Coast to the cold waters of Nova Scotia."

"An oyster aficionado," I said.

"For a buck a pop, they're fine. I'm Harrison Blanchard," he said and put out his hand.

He had a good grip. His hands were soft, but he held my hand hard.

I looked past him at the two women who'd given him nothing. He'd been trying and they'd been ignoring, looking around, hoping no one would think they were with the fat man. The alcohol was kicking in and I could see everything.

"What happened to your hands?" the man said.

I hadn't expected that. I finished my drink to get my clear vision back.

"I hit walls sometimes, but they're healed."

"Not completely," he said. "I'm a doctor. I've seen hands like that on fighters."

"I fight walls and I lose. Which makes me not much of a fighter."

"Bad anger management?"

"Only when I drink. Watch out."

The fat man looked me over. His face seemed to relax and his eyes didn't look so squinty.

"Are you free tonight?" he said.

"Free," I said and smiled.

"Are you?"

"It depends on the plan."

"Here's the plan," the fat man said. "Dinner is on me if you can get these two women to go out with us. I'll throw in a room at The Plaza if you can get them back to the hotel with us."

"Is that where you're staying?"

"I always stay at The Plaza when I'm in New York City. It reminds me of another time."

"Why not pick them up yourself? Flash them some cash, rich man."

"I don't like to do that."

"Then just talk. See where it goes naturally."

"Look at me."

I looked at him.

"I could talk like Shakespeare and it wouldn't matter."

"If you talked like Shakespeare, you could bed them."

"Most women sitting in bars don't want to talk to me. They think I'll cut into their chances of meeting a man who looks like you."

"So that's the challenge."

"It's more than a challenge. It's an impossibility. If I'm to have any chance of picking them up, I'll need some help. Are you game?"

"I'm done with challenges. All my future challenges will be imposed on me."

"Well then, let me impose on you," he said.

It made sense in a way. He could be a symbol, the fat man as prison. The fat man as the system that would keep me locked up for three years. If I could fulfill the fat man's challenge, maybe prison wouldn't be as bad as I thought it would be, wouldn't be as scary, wouldn't be as impossible. Three years. It was impossible. But if I fulfilled his challenge maybe prison would have toilets with doors that closed where I could shit in peace. It was drunk thinking. I signaled the bartender, ordered.

"I'll pick up your bar tab too," the fat man said.

"Yes you will."

The martini came.

"Put this on his tab," I said to the bartender and downed my drink in three gulps.

I leaned over the bar so I could look directly at the two women. They were having a scintillating conversation, or at least they didn't break eye contact with each other, but then they started laughing, and the woman facing me finally faced me, eyes on eyes, and I lifted my empty glass.

"It's empty," she said on cue.

"Let's have one together," I said. "My friend says he'll take care of us."

"I did?" The fat man lifted his eyebrows in mock surprise. I gave him credit for holding up his end. He was quick and his smile was charming, framed by two deep dimples. I could see him calming his patients before he laid his fat hands on them.

"Didn't you?" I said.

"Of course. It must have slipped my mind. Yes, drinks are on me. My name's Harrison by the way."

The women smiled. They were both turned around now, facing me, and the one who hadn't yet spoken held my eyes long enough for me to know. Her bed. My bed. It didn't matter. Sometimes it was that easy. I was supposed to be at Wendi's for dinner in less than an hour, but the challenge was on, a challenge I wouldn't get in prison. And I was buzzed. And time had slowed. And I could almost pull down my pants, squat, and take a shit with the whole bar watching. Almost.

The bartender put the drinks in front of us and we started talking. I didn't tell them what I did. I didn't interrogate them with biographical questions. We just talked. The one who'd looked long enough wore a turquoise bracelet and I told her I'd seen that color turquoise in New Mexico and the conversation went from there to deserts we'd seen to trips we'd taken to Paul Bowles and how he always wrote about deserts, a turn that surprised me, I hadn't pegged them as lit students getting their graduate degrees, and Harrison told a story about visiting a Bedouin camp in the Sinai and the pleasure of eating lamb with his hands, and Harrison ordered more drinks and more oysters, and I checked my watch and had two minutes to meet Wendi and less than five days of freedom and the women were laughing and Harrison was laughing and time slowly moved and slowly moved some more and it was time. Time to close the deal. I leaned forward.

"Listen," I said to the two women. "You're not going to be studying tonight and I'm not going to be taking any trips tonight and Harrison is tired of buying drinks and he's in no mood to eat with his hands like a Bedouin, so why don't we get out of here before happy hour ends and get some dinner. The Strip House is a few blocks away. If you haven't eaten there, their steaks are great. Harrison said he'd take care of us."

"I did?" Harrison said and we all laughed.

"It must have slipped my mind," he said.

The two women didn't protest too much. There was me, so it wouldn't look like they were dating the fat man, and they were enjoying Harrison's company. And they were buzzed.

Harrison signed off on his credit card and we all got up, easy for the three of us, a production for Harrison. He was even bigger standing up. His thighs were thick and his belly hung over his pants, and his torso was three man-widths across. He was tall too, taller than me. He breathed heavy, from the fat and the alcohol and maybe the expectation of a big steak dinner. He put his hand on my shoulder, gave me a quick wink, and we started walking the few blocks south and east to the Strip House.

The Strip House was all red, red walls and red leather banquets that looked from another time and pictures of old-time strippers everywhere. I'd been to some of the best steak houses in the city. This place was the best. The meat was salted and grilled perfectly, the creamed spinach was rich, the goose fat potatoes richer. I wouldn't be getting goose fat potatoes in prison. I heard they cooked everything with lard.

The maître d's eyes went wide seeing Harrison. There was a crowd at the bar, and there would be a long wait for a table, but Harrison was larger than life, a celebrity of genetic proportions, and the maître d' was smart. He knew Harrison would bottleneck the bar, and the women were good-looking enough to be almost eye-candy, and I knew I was looking good, my eyes alive from alcohol, my body in shape from doing hundreds of sit-ups and push-ups and pull-ups every day like I was preparing for a fight, which I was, five days to the opening round. My stomach was perfectly flat from having taken a great shit, a private shit, at Wendi's place before I left. I hit my stomach. I took it. I hit it again. Like a fight. Like a race. I could come up with so many Likes but already knew, felt, saw the way I could see things drunk, prison wouldn't be like anything. It would be itself. My hand was a fist. I opened my fingers. I was supposed to be at Wendi's. She was making pesto for me. I was with a fat man and two women, a great steak meal ahead of us, and in five days I'd be alone anyway and maybe, drunk-seeing, maybe this needed to be part of my preparation too, beyond working out, beyond shitting. I'd need to put everyone away and walk through the locked-down corridors of Bare Hill Correctional with dead eyes.

The maître d' took us straight to a back table. Harrison waited for the three of us to slide into the red booth before sitting himself down on a chair. We ordered cocktails. We ordered steaks. We drank. We talked. We laughed. We ate. We ordered dessert. My stomach was full of meat, meat that took a long time to digest.

Harrison was telling a story about a fellow doctor at his convention who admitted he passed out at the sight of blood, who couldn't even order a rare steak for fear he'd go down. They all laughed. I pictured Harrison in a white coat, stethoscope around his neck, taking vitals with his fat fingers. My drunk was turning. I didn't want these women. I didn't want to be this full. I didn't want the alcohol buzz to leave me, to move from happy to angry, how I got in trouble in the first place, kicking the shit out of some bartender who'd talked too much. I didn't want time, time before the other time started, to pass so fast.

Harrison was talking. The women were laughing. They were all having fun.

"What kind of doctor?" I said.

"I did?" Harrison said and the women laughed. It wasn't that funny.

"What kind of doctor are you?"

"Has everyone digested their food?" Harrison said. He was focused on the women. He was thinking he had a real shot. He could always get a hooker, but two free women for all night was more fun. I could see right through Harrison's eyes, right to his thoughts.

"What kind?" I said.

He turned to me, smiled, his eyes squinty and red.

"I'm a gastroenterologist. I'm a stomach doctor. Amply qualified, don't you think? I specialize in stomach staplings. I take fat people and make them less fat."

His smile went away.

"Don't ask," he said. "It's the obvious question. With me, it's biological. It's in my thyroid, not my stomach. When patients see me, they relax. It's all relative, right? I've only met two men bigger than I am, two men who came into my office, and now they lead normal lives, have wives and children and by all reports are happy."

Some of the anger went out of me.

"Tell me something," I said.

"Is it an obvious question?"

"It's a personal question. And since I won't ever see you again, and since I won't see the Strip House for at least three years, I'll ask it."

"Why won't you see the Strip House for three years?" Harrison said.

The women were listening, but they'd become background, as much a part of the table as the waiters and busboys moving around, out there somewhere.

"I'm going to prison."

"For what?"

"Obvious question," I said.

"What happens if you can't go to the bathroom?" I said.

"You die," Harrison said.

"What if it's in your head?"

Harrison put his fat hands flat on the table.

"If it's in your head, eventually you'll defecate. I've heard this many times before. When it concerns fecal matter, I've heard and seen it all. If it's in your head, your body will take over. The body always takes over. The body wins no matter what anyone says."

"What if I can't shit in there?"

"If you can shit here, you can shit there," Harrison said. His voice was even and calm, like he really had seen it all, and I believed he really was a doctor.

"I tell my patients to think of me," he said. "Pretend I'm sitting next to you. There's nothing you can do that would be more disgusting than what I look like. It's true. Think of me. I bet you could shit in front of me. I'll bet you the price of this steak dinner that you could shit in front of me."

"You're not the one I have to shit in front of," I said.

I turned to the women.

"He took you out to dinner. He kept you entertained. He's staying at The Plaza and if you're good, if you're true, you'll go back there with him. That's your sentence if you want to think of it that way. That's the way I think of things these days."

The women didn't say anything. But they were listening.

I shook Harrison's hand.

"Thanks for dinner," I said. "I'm full."

"That's a good start," Harrison said and smiled.

I walked out of the Strip House. I left the glowing red for the gray sidewalk. I was looking down, like looking for money, like looking for the sparkle in the concrete, like counting the squares, like counting. Three years. I'd tried counting one second per day and it took too long. One day per day was too much to think about.

I walked to Wendi's apartment.

I was drunk.

I stood in front of her building. I focused, remembered, pressed 2B. She buzzed me in without asking who I was. She had five more days with me. Closer to four really. She could live with me or without me. When she opened the door I smelled pesto. She didn't ask where I'd been.

"I could have called," I said.

I almost wanted to fight. I almost wanted to ruin it. I'd tell myself it was practice and just walk out. I'd been tired of all the nothing in my life before I met her. She was something. She had taken me right in.

"Are you hungry?" she said.

"Why wouldn't I be hungry? It's late."

"You smell like meat," she said. "When I was a kid, whenever our dog ate meat, my parents didn't let him stay in the house that night because he smelled. That's how you smell."

"What else do I smell like?"

She looked hard at me. Not angry-hard. Like she was studying me. Like she was assessing whether I was worth the fight or not.

"You don't smell like pussy," she said.

"Fear," she said. "You smell a little like fear. Like when you're sitting on the pot and can't shit because all these criminal motherfuckers are going to be watching you like in a nightmare."

"Thanks."

"I can re-boil the water," she said. "Or not."

"That was always my favorite scene in that movie."

"What movie?"

"I can't remember the name. This man and woman meet in a bar and she takes him home and about four in the morning he wakes up starving. The woman makes him a bowl of pasta carbonara. Just like that. Pasta carbonara from scratch. That was true love."

"No. That was love for the moment."

"Same thing."

"No. Love is about time."

"Don't tell me about time. I don't want to think about time."

"You'll learn about time soon enough," Wendi said.

"Stop."

48

"If you want to cut these last days short, that's fine. Five days will go that fast," she said and snapped her fingers in my face.

"I'm going to make these days last forever."

"How?"

"I'll keep drinking."

"Then you'll pass out, wake up hungover, sleep in, and you'll have lost a whole day. That's twenty percent of your time."

"Stop," I said.

My stomach turned over. Sometimes meat did that to me. Like a symbol. Substantial food went right through me, as if I weren't substantial enough to hold it. It was supposed to stay in my system, but my system didn't let it stay. Drinking was like a puzzle sometimes. Through drunken eyes, random pieces fit. Like running into a fat gastroenterologist. Like meat not sticking to my stomach. Like meeting Wendi when I needed to meet her. My stomach turned over again.

"Did you hear that?"

"You'll be fine," she said.

"I met a fat man tonight. He told me what to do. He told me to think of him sitting next to me. He was a stomach doctor. He told me my body would take over and I'd just shit."

"Exactly," Wendi said.

"It's my head. I see all these pictures. I see all these scenes. I wish I was in there already. I wish I was there so I'd only see what there is to see."

"You'll be fine," she said.

"I'm not that tough," I said.

"No one's that tough."

"I'm not that tough," I said and my stomach turned over.

I walked into the bathroom. I left the door open like an invitation. I pulled down my pants and sat on the pot.

Wendi came in and sat on the bathmat. She looked at me. I looked at her. I didn't let myself look away. They would look. I would look back. I would have to look back. I thought about the fat man. I thought about shitting in front of Harrison. I kept my eyes open on Wendi.

"You'll be fine," she said.

My asshole opened up. It was shit. It was just shit. It was just shit and I shit it, the shit hitting the water. Wendi watched me. She didn't blink. She didn't say a word. I ripped some toilet paper. I wiped my ass. There was a book of matches on the sink, next to a candle, for exactly this. It was a traveling trick. If the bathroom, if the outhouse, if the squat toilet stunk, a lit match made the stink disappear. I lit a match. I dropped it between my legs. It hit the water with a hiss and the smell was gone.

I'd have to find a match somewhere. A match that made three years disappear.

Wendi stood up from the bathmat and kissed me once on the lips, hard.

extra

For the last shot they put me far down the boardwalk. The day's ending. The horizon's pink and gray and the waves no longer look lazy with the tide coming in and the water rougher, darker. On the other side of the boardwalk the actor's trailer looks too new, too white.

They call places.

The actor walks out of the trailer. Even in the fading light the actor's eyes are still there, still lit. I'm watching him and he catches me. I don't move my eyes until he moves his, has to move his, he's the one walking, I'm not, have to be honest, the take hasn't started, and he walks easy and strong like the end of a movie, like a scene that should be my scene.

I blur my eyes, make the people watching him my extras.

It's getting cool, wind off the ocean. I button the vest they've made me wear. I just want to take the charter bus back to the city, back to my apartment to sleep. Tomorrow I have a 7 a.m. call for another day of extra work on another film.

The assistant director calls Action. I walk. In front of me the Ferris Wheel's still turning.

They do another take.

Another.

Another.

Another.

The assistant director calls That's a wrap.

It's almost dark.

The actor's walking toward me. People surround him and he keeps stopping for selfies. A woman pushes through, touches his shoulder. The actor's in front of me.

"Thanks for the day," he says.

"You're welcome."

"You were looking at me like you wanted to kill me," the actor says and smiles and I'm looking in his eyes, looking to see if I can learn something, something about how he is where he is, but I already know and his eyes move and he's walking and all around they're taking down the lights.

the aloha state

It wasn't our honeymoon, but it was Hawaii. It had been all
sky and water for thousands of miles, blue above, blue below. Then the
plane banked right and made its final approach to Oahu. In the baggage
claim area, a woman sold purple-flowered leis, wishing every passen-
ger Aloha as if she meant it. The woman, old and flat-featured, wore
an oversized Hawaiian shirt patterned with flowers and an old pair of
Nike high tops that looked three sizes big. She caught me looking at her
Nikes and the smile left her eyes.

The shuttle bus from the airport to Waikiki was too hot, too
filled with tourists already taking pictures of palms and ocean. We
weren't strangers here. My new wife had been to Honolulu many times
for work and I'd lived up on one of the city's tropical hills with my
parents, twenty years ago. It was the first time we were here together.
The island looked familiar but not completely. My kid eyes had become adult eyes. The clouds over the mountains were heavy and dark,
but above the ocean the sky was clear and the surfers were out, sitting
around, waiting for waves. In unison, all the cameras pointed left. A
double rainbow arced, greeting us to the island on cue.

My wife checked in while I stayed with the bags. She'd
planned the trip, she'd be working some of the days while I sunned
and swam, and I was never good with details anyway. Booking flights
and rooms and restaurants was her territory. Before that, she found the
apartment we moved into together, checked the requirements for a civil

marriage ceremony, and set up a small wedding dinner where our families met. I did the physical work. Packing up and loading boxes for the move. Lifting luggage for the trip. We'd each packed a bag of clothes and she'd filled a bag with things for work and I stood by the three bags while I surveyed the hotel's lobby. Japanese people with sunburns walked by, most with kids in tow, cute kids with circular, symmetrical faces. The man behind the check-in desk punched information into his computer, and Donna turned to me and smiled. She seemed happy to be here, happy to be here with me, to show me the Hawaii she'd come to know over several trips. I promised to show her the house where I'd lived as a kid. After Oahu, we'd go to the Big Island to see the volcanoes. She'd rent the car and I'd do the driving.

Donna slipped the room key into the slot and I brought the bags in and put them on the king-sized bed so we could unpack. It was a big, nondescript room, with beige carpeting, homogenized abstracts on the walls, and a set of off-white lamps, one on each side of the bed.

Donna slid open the glass door and walked onto the balcony.

"They weren't kidding," she said. "They told me the room had a partial view of the ocean."

I went out on the balcony and leaned over the rail to catch a sliver of Pacific.

"At least we have an unobstructed view of the Marriott's generators," I said.

"It's not so bad," Donna said.

"Not at all. It's Hawaii. Aloha."

"Aloha." She kissed me once and smiled. "I love how Aloha means hello and goodbye and also peace. Aloha. It sounds serene, doesn't it? Let's take a walk on the beach."

We had that airplane film on our skin, bad air and bad food and sitting too long without moving. We changed pants for shorts, shoes for flip-flops, and went down to catch the sunset.

Waikiki was crowded with tourists, more crowded than I remembered. My family had come to the beach almost every afternoon after school. We weren't from Hawaii so the possibility of lying on sand and listening to ocean felt like a year-long vacation. My father was on an exchange program at the University of Hawaii and my mother was teaching composition courses to make a few extra dollars and I attended a city school where I immediately learned that *Haole* meant *White* and Whites were a minority. During the school day I hated Hawaii. But at the beach, sitting in the sun with my parents and looking at the horizon, the mainland a straight shot across the water, everything felt okay again. In school, I would watch the second hand move on the watch my parents gave me and count down the minutes to afternoon, to Waikiki Beach. I learned to surf at Waikiki. I learned to swim strong. My skin turned dark, my blond hair bleached, and Japanese tourists offered my parents money to take my photograph. I looked like an All-American kid, a happy and healthy towhead.

Donna and I took off our flip-flops and walked through the sand. The sand felt good, just to walk felt good after the flight. I breathed in the ocean air. I stepped into the foam of a breaking wave. The last fight we'd had in New York felt five thousand miles away, which it was.

"Do you remember Waikiki?" she said.

"I think we used to set up our towels in front of that pink hotel."

Across the water the surfers crowded around each other and waited for waves. I remembered needing to paddle my board out a mile to get to the breaking waves, but now saw they broke a hundred yards out.

"And I used to surf there. Unless the reefs move every few years."

"Every few years or every twenty years?" she said.

"Thanks."

"Mahalo," Donna said. "Aloha. Mahalo. Luau. Lei. Hawaiian words you need to remember. And no, reefs don't move that quickly."

"Haole. Don't forget Haole. No matter how tan I got, I was still a Haole."

Like a ritual, almost everyone on the beach stood to watch the sunset. It was late August and the man next to us extended his arm and pointed at the sun setting into the water.

"See how it's falling in the ocean and not the mountain ridge? That means summer's coming to an end," he said and walked away.

"It feels right," I said.

"What feels right?" Donna said.

"That everyone stands for the sun."

As soon as the sun touched the water, it seemed to move double-time.

People all around were taking pictures. They wouldn't come out well. I could see some of the pictures they were taking. Distances never came out well, not unless they were shot by pros.

The top of the sun burned hard for a moment and was gone, the sky lighting up and then darkening, the blues turning slate, the quiet pinks turning neon and fading, and by the time the darkest slates pressed the horizon most of the people who had stood, who had photographed the day's end, were gone, off to shower, off to dinner. Donna and I stood quietly until the first stars became visible. With the sun and ocean and sky, with all the elements right there, I couldn't help thinking about time and space and nature's power. In New York, my big thoughts, the thoughts that came when I stopped, which wasn't often, were about people. The skyscrapers built, the technology developed, the constant movement of bodies down avenues, across streets, the dreams and plans of all those rushing, big dreams because they were New York dreams but not really big at all.

"Is that a planet or a star?" Donna said, pointing to the sky.

"It's a plane."

"It's not. It's not moving."

"I don't know. It looks pretty bright. It's probably a planet."

"I still remember our third-grade teacher crossing Pluto off our galaxy map. She told us how a congress of astronomers had voted to downgrade the planet. I thought that was kind of mean."

"It's a cruel universe," I said, and we walked back to the hotel.

It was late, we were tired, and Donna didn't feel like traveling to one of the restaurants where she usually ate, away from the Waikiki strip. We looked into a few places and settled on a burger and beer joint with an outdoor balcony. Below us, Tiki lamps flamed and palm fronds moved in the breeze. Across the avenue I could see a piece of ocean. Traffic was too heavy for beach sounds. We ordered Mai-Tais to get in the spirit and grilled mahi-mahi sandwiches instead of burgers.

"It feels exactly like 2 a.m.," I said.

"Very funny."

"What's the time difference again?"

"You know the exact time difference. That's why it feels exactly like 2 a.m."

"It's amazing, isn't it? You get on a plane in the morning and before the sun sets, you're thousands of miles away on a tropical island. And the sun stays out that whole time."

"The sun stays out all the time," Donna said. "We're the ones moving."

"When I was a kid, I thought if I kept traveling west, I could cheat time and live forever."

"That's a kid's thought. Are you going to have another Mai-Tai?"

"They're too sweet."

Donna called over the waiter and ordered another drink. I checked her eyes. It was mostly fruit juice.

"So," Donna said.

I waited.

"So, I rented bikes for us. Tomorrow we can ride past Diamondhead and I'll show you the coast. I don't have to work until seven."

"Sounds good."

"Pick an afternoon and you can show me where you used to live. Do you remember the address?"

"I remember the address. I just don't remember how to get there."

"Details," she said.

"I'll check at the front desk if they have a detailed map of Honolulu."

I pointed to a plumeria tree below us. We'd had one in our yard twenty years ago. White flowers, yellow centers, and I could almost smell their sweetness.

"I was looking for a plumeria," I said. "After dinner, I need to pick a flower. It's the best smell in the world."

Donna's Mai Tai came.

"Aloha," she said and lifted her cocktail.

It wasn't a steep hill, but it was a long hill. I followed Donna. I copied the gear she was in, second to lowest, and spun my legs as best

I could. She was a cyclist. I was a runner. Before we married, I said I'd start biking with her and the day after the court clerk declared us official, Donna bought me a road bike, sleek and silver. Some days we rode around Central Park's loop. Some days we rode along the Hudson. I preferred running and refused to get clip-in pedals, I didn't like being locked in, so I had to work extra hard, especially on the hills, while Donna pedaled effortlessly, her strong legs spinning in perfect arcs. On the hills she killed me. We stopped at the top of the climb and looked over the famous Hanauma Bay where I'd snorkeled as a kid. I'd learned the names of all the colorful fish and different kinds of coral. One choppy afternoon a dragon eel swam at me and I scrambled out of the water and ran across the coral, giddy with fear, my snorkel still in my mouth, back to my parents. They were sunbathing. My mom wore a pink bikini and my dad wore a red Speedo.

"They were around my age."

"Who was?" Donna said. She wasn't even breathing from the ride.

"My parents. They were around the age I am now when we lived here."

"Cool."

"It's strange to think about."

"That your parents were once your age?"

"They were adults in my eyes. I still feel like a kid."

"Maybe they felt like kids too."

"Maybe."

"You're not such a kid. You're married now. Remember?"

"They call that area just past the first reef the second level. I used to venture out there. The fish were better. I never went to the third level."

"The third level," Donna said like it held terrifying creatures.

Then she laughed. "I scuba dived here once. It wasn't like Australia. I saw dozens of sharks in Australia. It wasn't like Malaysia."

"I haven't been. But I was here."

I was, but I wasn't. I'd seen photographs of me on the island, thin-legged and thin-armed, standing next to my surfboard, or holding my snorkeling gear, or showing off a shell I'd just found. It was me, but it wasn't.

"Come on," Donna said. "We can ride to the blow hole from here. Do you remember the blow hole?"

"I don't."

"There's a hole in the lava. When the waves come in, sea spray blows out of the hole."

Donna clipped into her pedals and I followed, pushing down, my legs working hard, harder than her legs. I pictured getting off the bike, throwing it in the ocean so I could just run.

The next day, I spent the day alone. Donna had a long session that would take her into evening, we'd meet to eat, and she had another session at night.

I killed time, waiting for dinner. Before when I traveled, I'd travel with the woman of the month, so she was still new, or I'd travel alone, so I could meet new women. Traveling with my wife of six months, the woman I'd been with for almost a full year, was different.

I sat in the sun.

I swam.

I sat in the sun some more.

She was in the hotel room, working.

I walked on Waikiki Beach. I walked on Kalakaua Avenue, which bordered Waikiki. I asked the cashier at an ABC Store if the Ala Moana Center still existed. That was where we'd gone shopping, where we sometimes ate, where I bought my parents their anniversary gift that year. The cashier told me Ala Moana was still around, a few miles away, near the pier. Towel around my neck, sunglasses cutting the glare, I walked. It was hot, but no hotter than New York in the summer, and I looked left and right, left and right, seeing if what I saw and my memory aligned. I walked and I looked. I thought about my marriage and my parents' marriage. I thought about the kid in the photographs and me. I thought about reefs moving, growing, living creatures themselves.

Ala Moana was not how I remembered. The mall had been gutted and renovated, more shine, more glass. Twenty years. I walked the long, open mall and the loss came into my throat. The long time ago came into my throat. I'd been a kid. My parents had practically been kids. We were a young family spending a year in Hawaii. I walked up the stairs to the mall's second level and recognized the tallest building across the street and looked at the houses built on Oahu's hills and blurred my eyes.

That night we ate dinner in a Japanese place on Kalakaua Avenue, the only restaurant Donna said she liked on the Waikiki strip. I didn't know why we'd eaten in a burger place our first night. Maybe she hadn't been in the mood for sushi. We ate a lot of sushi in New York.

Donna ordered sake and looked over the menu.

"They serve a traditional Japanese breakfast here," she said. "I don't know if you'd like it."

"I might."

"It's clean. It's a good way to start the day. I ate here a lot last year."

I let her order the sushi and sashimi the way she always did.

She spoke some Japanese. I watched the tourists walking by, some tan, some red, burned by their first days in Hawaii. A lot of the tourists ate ice cream. A lot of them held name-brand shopping bags. The Tiki lamps burned and every few moments the flames lengthened, sucking at the tropical breeze for more oxygen.

"How was work?"

"My client needed constant attention," she said. "How was your day? What did you do?"

"I sat in the sun. I swam a little."

"You look good. You got some good color. Did you rent a snorkel?"

"No."

"There's a reef at the end of the beach. I told you."

"It's not as much fun alone. If I spot a rare fish, I'll have no one to show it to."

"You can tell me about it afterward."

The sushi came and we ate without talking. The first time we ate sushi together, Donna showed me the best way to mix wasabi into soy sauce, putting a little soy in the dish first, mixing up the paste, adding more soy for taste. It was a good trick. She said she was full and put down her chopsticks. I finished the rest of the rolls.

"I'm stuffed," she said. "I'm tired. One more session to go. He has a shoe fetish. I'm making him bring me a new pair of Manolo Blahniks as part of his tribute."

"When do you work tomorrow?"

"Early. And for most of the day. We can meet for a ride in the late afternoon."

"I feel like I haven't seen you in a while."

"You've seen me."

I didn't say anything.

"I told you this was going to be a work vacation. I told you if you didn't want to come, you didn't have to."

"You said you wanted me to come."

"You said you needed a vacation. You knew I'd be working. I wasn't going to tell you not to come. It was your choice."

"Nice," I said.

"Don't start that passive aggressive shit. I worked all day. I'm tired."

She signaled the waitress for the check, pulled out her stack of cash, and peeled off some twenties. She downed her sake. I hated when she drank. A few too many sips and her eyes changed.

"I have to go back to work soon."

"I know."

"I'll be done at ten. There are some decent bars farther down the strip if you feel like it."

"Cheers."

"We'll have four days on the Big Island together. I won't be working at all."

"I look forward to it."

"Good," she said, but her smile was far away and I didn't even bother pretending.

She woke before me. I heard her get out of bed, go into the bathroom. Then I felt her hand on my shoulder and then her fingers in my hair. She told me she had to start getting ready.

I got out of bed. I put on my bathing suit and the red surfing shirt I'd bought at the Billabong store. I got my towel and book and suntan lotion.

She was silent, putting on her makeup in the bathroom.

In our apartment building, in the city, a woman lived across the hall. She was pretty and blonde and athletic looking. I sometimes saw her coming out of the Equinox on Broadway, and she'd give me a nice smile. She had very straight teeth. She started dating a new man. For the first three weeks, we heard them in bed, loud. It was like clockwork. Between eleven and twelve they'd go at it and again between six and seven the next morning. Every night, every morning, for three weeks. Then the morning sessions became less consistent and then the night sessions and then the sounds lowered, lasted ten minutes or less, and by the end of two months we never heard them. That's how it was. Then the man stopped coming around. That had been me. I'd get bored and move on. With Donna it lasted longer. We were both moody and needy, but the exciting part stayed and forever became a word we could say without smirking. We were caught up. The plan was made. The papers were signed. The ceremony lasted a minute, but when we walked out of the courthouse that freezing winter morning, it all felt right. I knew it would change. She knew it would change. But it had lasted longer. Then it changed. I remembered other women, all those other women. And walking New York's streets there were all those women. I looked, never touched, felt stuck, less alive. After marriage, after kids, the next big event was death. Some nights it was nice to go home, our apartment a home or almost, have dinner, watch TV, relax, sleep comfortably. But there were nights when we didn't talk enough, didn't laugh enough, meals where we hardly said a word, pauses where I didn't know the woman in front of me and, I guessed, she didn't know me or want to know me. The fighting began. I almost hadn't made it to Hawaii.

I was ready to leave the hotel for the day. I looked at her. She was putting on mascara and looking at herself in the mirror. I walked to the door and opened it and waited for her to say something. She didn't. Her eyes were blank, the way they went when she drank, the way they went before work, like I wasn't there.

"Bye," I said.

"Bye. See you tonight."

"Is that it?"

"What do you want?"

"Nothing."

"I have to get ready for work."

"It's not the work."

"I wonder."

"That's too easy," I said.

She stood there, holding her mascara brush in front of her eye, looking at me in the mirror's reflection. I held the reflection of her eyes until I could feel the anger pushing me to start a new fight. It was too exhausting.

"Later," I said and closed the door.

The water was clear. The coral wasn't spectacular, but there were plenty of beautiful fish. I'd forgotten most of their names. I remembered the Parrotfish, its thick, colorful body and beak-like mouth. I remembered the Moorish Idol, an over-sized angel fish with yellow, black, and white stripes. I moved along the surface of the water slowly, looking through my mask. The sun lit the water and I could see everything.

It was easy swimming. The flippers made it even easier.

I saw movement against a rock and focused. I saw the movement again. It was an eel, body camouflaged, trying to work its way into a crevice. Only its movement made it different from the rock. I stayed where I was and watched. The body disappeared. I waited. Its head came out. It was a pre-historic head. Its eyes looked dead and its mouth stayed open. It was built to eat, to wait and watch and clamp its jaws together.

She woke before me.

I got out of bed. I put on my bathing suit and the red surfing shirt. I got my towel and book and suntan lotion.

I sat in the sun.

I swam.

I sat in the sun some more.

Before her evening session we took a bike ride together, in search of Ualakaa Street where my family had lived. I followed her along Honolulu's crowded streets to the hills. Donna obeyed traffic regulations, coming to a full stop and clipping out at red lights, signaling turns with her hand. If it were up to me, I'd just ride. It wasn't like Hawaii Five-O was going to pull my bike over and write me a ticket.

I hadn't checked the directions and the phone signal was weak. We had to keep stopping and asking people if they knew where Ualakaa Street was. We were on the right hill, near the private school, the Punahou School, that I remembered, where the rich mainlanders sent their kids, but we couldn't find Ualakaa. The higher up the hill we rode, the fewer people we saw. I pedaled hard to intercept a Japanese man out for a run. He didn't know the street. I pulled next to a car backing out of a driveway. The woman kept her window up. She didn't know the street. The hill was steep. My calves felt the incline.

"This is getting ridiculous," Donna said.

"We'll find someone who knows. It's here. I know it's close to here."

"Why didn't you look it up?"

"I just didn't."

"You had plenty of time."

"You're right. I've had plenty of time. All I've been doing is killing time."

"Tough life. You were lounging on Waikiki Beach and getting a tan. I feel very guilty about that."

"I'm not asking you to feel guilty."

"I don't."

"It's around here somewhere."

"I don't feel like wasting time riding up and down these hills. I want to ride along the coast. I only have a few hours off."

"What's the rush?"

"I have to work soon."

"I used to live here. I want to see the house."

"You should have checked where it was."

"I didn't," I said. "But I want to see the house."

"You can come back tomorrow. You'll have the whole day free."

"We're supposed to be a couple."

"What does that mean?"

"It means you're my wife. We're supposed to do things together."

"We do a lot of things together. I'm here to work."

"It's like we're not a real couple," I said. "We're not like it's supposed to be."

"How is it supposed to be?"

"Not like us."

And, the way she went more and more, she went off. Off on how she worked harder for our marriage than I worked, how she put in long hours for us, made money for us, how I didn't appreciate what she did. Every time we fought, she brought up what she did. What she did was beat people for a living. She was a famous dominatrix. Men and women hired her to bind them, beat them, deprive them of oxygen, flay them, put them in sensory deprivation bags, hang them upside down, insert dildos up their rectums. The first time we went out, Donna told me exactly what she did. She was honest and I wasn't fazed. It all seemed like so much game-playing and I preferred my sex to be real-raw. When a woman wanted me to hurt her, I used my hands. I didn't need props or costumes. Donna had some good stories, and we laughed about how I'd dominated the dominatrix, but her world wasn't that interesting to me. When she went to the S and M clubs to make an appearance, I was happy to let her go on her own. When she came back from work, I didn't ask about the details of her day. One night, I was out drinking with some guys I knew from work and, by chance, we passed the Limelight where they held the Black and Blue Ball, one of the big BDSM events. The line in front of the Limelight looked like a Halloween party for lost kids and out-of-shape adults, everyone dressed in their best black-and-blue costumes. There were lots of piercings, lots of tattoos, lots of leather and latex. The guys I was with laughed at the people on line. I laughed at the people in line. I didn't tell them my wife was inside. When we fought, Donna accused me of having a problem with what she did. I had no problem and that was the problem. Men paid to worship her, but to me, Donna was just Donna, the Donna I knew, the Donna who was my wife. That's what I'd tell her. It was the word *just* that pissed her off.

The street was steep. We were stopped. Holding our bikes. Standing. Donna clipped out of her pedals. Me in my running shoes.

Both of us still wearing our helmets. And Donna was telling me the same old, same old about her work. I waited until there was a break in the speech.

"I'm tired," I said.

"What are you tired about? I'm tired. I'm tired from working every day. I'm tired of being taken for granted."

"I'm tired of being married," I said.

She stood very still. Her eyes emptied, a different empty from after drinking or before working. I didn't recognize her, not really, and I didn't care.

"Maybe you're right," I said. "Maybe I'm the one who doesn't work hard enough at this. I still feel tired. I feel like I'm losing a piece of my life every day, day after day after day. I feel like I'm going to get old too fast."

She looked down, maybe at her hands on the handlebars. Her nails were painted red. She still scratched my back in bed, still held on tight, but my eyes would stay open and I'd stopped looking at her. It had become routine, not much more than doing push-ups on a mattress. I looked at her in front of me. She was very beautiful. Her lips were closed, and she smiled a sad smile.

"Isn't that what we're supposed to do?" she said. "Grow old together?"

"I don't know."

Her eyes didn't move for a long time.

"Why did you want this?" she said.

"We both wanted it."

"I had my life. You made me change my life and I did, more than you know. You didn't. Almost not at all."

"I don't even know who you are anymore."

"No," Donna said. "You don't."

Her voice was flat. It was the voice she used on clients. When we first started dating, I'd sometimes wait outside her studio, wait for her to be done, and sometimes I could hear her voice, low and flat and commanding.

"You never took the time to care who I was," she said.

She took a long breath. When she beat people, she told them to breathe into the pain. That way, they could take a little more, and a little more after that.

"So," she said. "So is this it?"

"I don't know."

"You don't know," she said, flat.

Her mouth was a straight line. Usually, when she biked, she smiled. She never looked happier than when she was clipped into her bike, riding fast, free and locked-in at the same time. I never felt happier than when I was alone and the night was ahead of me, free and young, me in my own movie, and I could do what I wanted. That was how I'd lived my life. My life before marriage. I'd tired of that life, I'd been ready for change, and now I was tired of my new life, my married life, tired of her, tired of the drama and the compromise and pretending we were a couple. And she was tired too. We'd taken it out of each other.

"You're too weak to know even that," she said.

"It's not about weak or strong."

"Tell yourself what you need to tell yourself. I'm much stronger than you."

"You're not in your dungeon now," I said. "I'm not one of your sniveling slaves. Your pretend-strength means nothing to me."

"At least they can take it."

"They want to take it."

"There comes a point when they think they can't, but they do."

I pictured it, put the picture away.

"Whatever," I said. "It always sounds like a big game to me."

"You wouldn't know. You have no idea what I do."

"I have no interest in what you do. It's not about what you do. It's you. You go away. And I go away."

"You've stopped coming back," she said.

She looked down at her hands or her cycling shoes or the road. I couldn't tell.

"You see the bad in everything," she said. "I bought you a bike and you hate it. I try to make our home a home and you hate it. I kiss you and you hate it, like you're in a cage and need to get out."

"That's you. I don't work with cages."

"That's right. That's me. Deal with it."

"I do. It's trivial to me."

"I know."

We stood there. I looked up the hill. I sort of recognized the street but not really. I didn't know where it was. I hadn't looked it up. I figured I'd find it, remember it, twenty years disappearing, the street and the memory of the street lining up, but I didn't really know where I was.

Donna took another long breath.

"You couldn't take it," she said. "You couldn't take marriage."

I didn't say anything. She looked broken and I didn't really care.

"You never loved me," she said.

"I did love you."

"You loved the falling in love. That's the easy part. Kids fall in love all the time. That's what you loved. I was caught up in that too, but I loved you," she said.

She took another breath.

"The easy part," she said, like she was talking to herself.

"Maybe I like the easy part."

"The easy part is easy."

I felt my eyes narrow.

"I was never enough," she said. "How come I was never enough?"

"You were enough at the beginning."

She didn't have to say the word again. It was there. Easy.

Donna was looking straight at me.

She took a long breath and let it out slow.

"I'm going to go," she said.

"I don't want you here with me," she said. "I don't want you coming to the Big Island with me. I don't want to see your face. You're poison. You've poisoned me."

Her voice broke, but her mouth, her eyes stayed hard. I could see her controlling herself.

She turned the bike and faced it downhill. She swung her leg over the bar, clipped in, and started pedaling. I watched her move away, her legs spinning effortlessly. I watched her raise her arm, signal her turn, and then I couldn't see her anymore.

I stood there. I didn't move. I had the urge to call her, to call her back the way she'd called me back many times. I didn't.

There would be a lot of details. I'd have to change my flight. I'd have to pack. I'd have to find an apartment. I'd have to let my parents know my marriage was over. And I'd have to start going out like I'd gone out. I'd have to do that.

There was no one on the street, no one to ask directions. I didn't care. That self-destructive not-caring, that kid not-caring. I didn't need to see where I'd lived. It had been a bad year. A bad year now. A bad year then. When people heard I'd lived in Hawaii, they said how great that must have been. They didn't know. I'd been a haole in a new school. I'd counted seconds on my watch until the day was done. I'd hated so much about Hawaii when I'd been here twenty years ago. Fuck the house. It was easier just to bike back to Waikiki. Our flight to the Big Island was in the morning. Her flight now. Maybe I'd just sleep on the beach, get my things from the room after she left, maybe spend another day in Honolulu, darken my tan so when I got back to the city I'd look healthy for a while.

I rode down the hill.

I rode to the beach.

I put the bike down on the sand and sat there. Waikiki.

The sun moved down the sky.

I watched the surfers. My parents had probably watched me, their blond kid waiting for waves. I'd never love anyone as much as I'd once loved my parents. She knew it. She'd said as much, flat-voiced and drunk one night.

The sun moved faster at the end. And the big thoughts started coming in. Death thoughts. Maybe it was the clouds that were now pink-tipped, looking like angels facing west. Maybe it was the obvious, the setting sun, the end of the day. I sometimes wondered how I'd face the end. If I were sick, if I were tired and in pain, maybe I'd be brave. Maybe I'd raise my arms and try to fight with nothing to lose. If I were healthy, like I was, I wouldn't be brave. I already knew that. When I got back to the city, I'd start rushing again, rushing through women, rushing through drunk nights so I wouldn't have to think, all easy, so the alcohol and new beds would help me believe I was living, really living, me in my movie.

The sun was almost down. Everyone around me was standing, looking west, cameras poised, ready to take the shot, but I stayed sitting.

"Aloha," I said.

black belt

The post said this:

We are looking for a karate teacher for three afternoons/week after 3:00 to teach a sweet 7 yr. old autistic boy for approx. 1 hour. He has had a tiny bit of experience but is eager and able to learn. Child will have a shadow therapist. Experience with special needs/autism helpful and preferred though not absolutely necessary. An open mind and a patient heart required. Please respond with resume and references as well as your fee. Thank you for your responses.

My mind wasn't open, my heart wasn't patient, but a rich family willing to shell out money for their messed-up kid might connect me to other rich families with other messed-up kids. If I played it right, I could start a little martial arts business, make some easy money, be my own boss.

The post asked for a resume, so I wrote one up. I didn't list my own special needs. I didn't list the bars and restaurants I'd worked in, short stints that often ended badly. Instead, I created a professional life. BA in Psychology. Magna cum laude, of course. MA in Special Education. I figured no one would ask to see actual diplomas. Present Experience: Part-time karate instructor at Equinox. A woman I knew worked at the sports club and said she'd vouch for me if I promised to take her out to dinner. Past Experience: Phys. Ed. teacher at The Giving School in Seattle. An old friend had moved west and was willing to lie. I told him to answer to Dr. Jonathan Esiason. His Seattle area code would make him sound real.

I wrote a quick note, attached my resume, and a week later a woman called. She asked some questions about my teaching methods (I said my methods were Montessori-based yet cutting-edge), my level of patience (I said I'd grown up with three younger siblings and had done my graduate internship in a kindergarten), my experience with autism (I hesitated, but the half-packed boxes in my apartment spurred me on. I knew autistics rocked a lot. I knew they didn't focus. I didn't know anything else. But that's not what I said. I said I understood an autistic child's special needs, that I'd tailor my karate instruction to her son, that individual tutoring was the cornerstone of The Giving School's mission and The Giving School was considered a model school in Seattle.) The woman said I sounded perfect. She said Dr. Esiason had given me a glowing recommendation. She said Dr. Esiason hoped I'd return to Seattle soon to resume my stellar teaching career. I told the woman that Dr. Esiason was very kind, but I had my own dreams, my own visions. I wanted to start my own school right here in Manhattan, a karate school for special children, a place where physical activity would break learning barriers and remove social stigmas and create an education-friendly environment where confidence could be built, brick by learning-challenged brick. The woman said that sounded like a wonderful plan. She asked when I could start working with her son.

Before my first session I bought a gi. I'd already taken out a martial arts book from the library, memorized a few stances, practiced some basic katas. I figured I didn't need to learn much. The kid wouldn't know the difference between a well-executed roundhouse and a karate-movie move, and whoever the shadow was, whatever a shadow was, I guessed they were no black belt. I put on my gi, crisp and white, looked in the mirror, bowed formally, introduced myself to me as Marcus-san. I imagined rustling bamboo and whistled a Japanese-sounding tune, something I remembered from *You Only Live Twice*. I narrowed my eyes and said in my best dubbed-over English, You have shamed my family, and now you must pay with ultimate price. I pushed the sound from my gut. HiiiYaaa.

It was a doorman building, of course. The post said money— private lessons, autistic kid, shadow therapist. Shadows had to cost money. The doorman asked my name, picked up the phone, made the call, announced my name, put down the phone, pointed me to the elevator. Another doorman, same blue uniform, same subservient hat, stood by the elevator. I walked in first. He followed. It was an old-fashioned elevator with a sliding gate and a rolling handle the operator really had to operate. I liked the sound the gate made, accordion of well-oiled metal, when the doorman pulled it shut. He rolled the handle and we started up.

"How's the kid?" I said.

"The Brandt boy?"

"Right. How's the Brandt boy?"

"Have you met the Brandt boy?"

"First time," I said.

The doorman stopped the elevator with a jolt, his hand fast on the handle. The elevator floor and the twelfth-floor floor were lined up, perfectly.

"This is you," the doorman said.

"Good job. Maybe a quarter inch off."

The elevator operator was paid not to say *Fuck you*. And *Fuck you* wouldn't have sounded right with the subservient hat he was wearing. I walked out of the elevator and into the hall. The gate closed hard behind me, oiled metal, pulley working, going down.

There was one door in the hall. In my apartment, the one I'd shared with my wife, there were four apartments per hall and enough room to stretch, at least a little, in the hallway. In the building I lived before I got married, there were sixteen apartments per hall, A through P. I'd been in D, between a fifty-something social worker with wild, wiry gray hair and a retired locksmith who left his apartment once a day to visit the downstairs liquor store. I was headed back there, back to broke, back to cramped halls, sad people, liquor store visits, unless my karate business boomed.

"Boom," I said out loud and rang the doorbell.

I waited. I heard steps. It could be the mother. It could be the shadow. I doubted it would be the kid. I had my gym bag slung over my shoulder, gi inside, a fake black belt I'd cut from an old pair of waiter pants. The scissors had frayed the material, but if anyone asked, I'd say it was my original belt from when I was a kid.

The door opened. She wasn't beautiful, but she was close. Even features. Full lips. Straight teeth. Chestnut-colored hair to her shoulders. A slim, fit body. She wore jeans and a T-shirt that looked expensive, the denim dark blue, the cotton of her shirt softer looking than the Hanes T's I wore.

"I'm Corey's mother."

She turned to look behind her. I took her in.

"I'll be right there," she said. Her voice was patient, soothing.

She turned back to me and I looked at her eyes. They were kind eyes and they were tired. And they were sad. I have a strange reaction when women cry in front of me. My cock goes hard. It's not a protective thing. It's not a dominant thing. Maybe it's because they're as close as they come to coming without being in bed. The veil of adulthood, of being careful, of mature control is removed, and, crying, they're open, sometimes more open than if their legs were spread before me. Her eyes took me in, and I shifted my gym bag to cover my crotch.

I changed in the bathroom and walked out wearing my gi, frayed black belt tied around my waist.

"This way." Her voice, farther down the hall, was tired too.

The wood floors shone, polished almost slippery, cool against my bare feet. I walked down the hall to a room that had been set up as a dance studio. Maybe she had danced. Three of the walls were mirrored. One wasn't. Along it, waist level, was a ballet bar.

She was standing there.

Her kid was standing next to her, head down, looking at the floor.

"This is Corey," she said.

"Hi Corey. I'm Marcus." I almost said Sensei Marcus like I'd practiced in the mirror, and I would have said Sensei, would have bowed, would have pushed the charade if Corey's mother wasn't standing next to him.

"And this is Dr. Parness."

Dr. Parness sat in a chair in the far corner of the room. She wore khakis and a buttoned blouse and glasses with wire frames. There was nothing vivid about her face. Plain features. Unexpressive mouth. Her hair was between blond and brown, cut short. I assumed she was the shadow.

I nodded my head for her, karate-style.

I looked back at Corey's mother. She smiled, sort of. It seemed a gesture of politeness, nothing more.

"Is there anything you need?"

"I'm ready to go," I said.

She turned to her son. "Your first day of karate lessons, Corey. It's exciting."

The kid didn't say anything.

"This is what you wanted. Marcus is going to be your karate teacher."

Corey's mother stepped back a step and I could see the kid's jaw tighten.

"It's fine," she said. "I'll be in the kitchen. I'm going to make you a special dinner to celebrate your first day of karate."

She took another step back. "Enjoy your lesson, sweetheart."

Corey's mother left the room. The shadow stayed. Corey was looking at the floor.

"Let's start by stretching," I said. "Even the greatest karate masters need to stretch before they begin."

I had to go over every stretch piece by piece. I had to say everything slowly and do everything slowly so he could do what I did slowly. After we stretched, we worked on a basic stance. I had to think about breaking everything down into pieces. I spread one leg and told him to spread one leg. I spread my other leg and told him to spread his other leg, just like I was doing. I made one hand into a fist and told him to make his hand into a fist. I made my other hand into a fist and told him to make his other hand into a fist. I put one fist at my side. I put the other fist at my side. The way we were moving, he'd have his black belt at seventy.

At the end of the lesson, I stood right in front of the kid, squared off with him as if he were the mirror. His head was still down. I didn't whistle the Bond movie theme song. I didn't throw any punches or attempt a flying kick. I held my hands out, palms flat, at Corey's eye level. He didn't look up, at my face or my palms. He was always look-ing down, not at his feet but at a space just beyond his feet, like he was looking for coins on the street, but not intently. It wasn't a blank stare, but it wasn't a stare of interest, of action.

"I'm here," I said.

He didn't say anything, of course.

"I'm here. My hands are here. It's called hand-eye coordina-tion. What I want you to do is ball your hands into fists and hit my hands."

He didn't move. I could sense the shadow stirring. Maybe she thought this was dangerous, me getting too close to the kid, me insti-gating actual contact. I hadn't looked at the shadow once during the session. For all her shadow therapy, the kid was still a mess.

"You want to be a karate fighter, right? You want to earn your belts and move up in the karate world. You're going to have to hit somebody some time, so we might as well start today. No time like the present, right, kid?" I caught myself. "Right, Corey?"

Corey nodded his head, but not like a normal kid, enthusias-tically, an exaggerated up and down, the way I thought a normal kid would nod. I didn't have too much contact with kids. I didn't have any contact with kids. I didn't even like kids. But there was a slight move-ment, a slight up from the usual down position.

"Go on, ball up your hands. Make your hands into fists, just like I showed you."

I watched his small hands become smaller, tighter.

"Good. Excellent. Now look up, look at my palms, and when you're ready, throw that punch right at one of my palms."

Corey didn't move.

"He doesn't like to touch things," she said. Her voice wasn't high-pitched or low. It wasn't loud and it wasn't quiet. It was monotone, each word the same dull note.

I looked at the shadow therapist, nodded my head.

"You speak?"

"I do speak," she said. "Getting Corey acclimated to making actual physical contact will take some time."

"No time like the present," I said. "Haven't you been listening?"

I took Corey's wrist in my right hand. I felt the resistance but held him firm and forced his fist forward into my left palm. It was a weak smack, more of a tap, but it made a little noise. I held his wrist, moved his arm back, pulled his fist forward again, harder. This time there was the pleasing snap of skin on skin. I pulled his fist forward, harder. The snap was louder, sharper.

"Good. That's good. It's a nice sound too. The harder you hit, the cleaner the sound, the sharper the snap. I know you like the way that sounded. Now you try."

I let go of the kid's wrist. His hand was still a fist.

"Go on. Right into my palm."

He stood there. His head was still down. I saw him breathing. He was breathing a little faster. That's all. He didn't move.

I looked at the shadow. She had that professional smugness, that tight-lipped, told-you-so look. My wife never looked smug even when she was right. My wife's lips never went tight like that. Sometimes my wife screamed. She'd scream and I'd scream back. I felt like screaming at the kid. To hit me. To hit me hard. To prove that his shadow didn't know what the fuck she was doing. I breathed.

"Okay, kid. Okay, Corey. Next time. You think about making a fist and hitting my palm. You think about making that nice sound. You can even practice punching in the mirror. You can pretend. And you'll only be hitting air and air can't get hurt. And don't worry about hurting my palm. I have strong hands. And you saw it doesn't hurt your fist. You have strong hands too. So think about that and next time we'll do it."

Corey stood there, eyes to the floor.

"All right. That's the end of today's lesson. I'll see you in two days."

I stepped back from the kid and bowed once. He wasn't looking at me, but he must have seen me. He bowed back, not exaggerated, not a full down, full up, but it was a bow, sort of.

I walked around the apartment a lot, talking to myself. It wasn't our apartment anymore. It was the apartment. She'd bought all the new furniture, so that was gone. And she was gone. She'd found a sublet on West End Avenue. It was April. Our lease, the lease she'd responsibly signed, ran out the last day of May. I had to be gone in six weeks.

It was mostly empty space, a lot of floor surface, planks of wood that still looked new. They'd redone the floors before we'd moved in. We were going to build a new life on new floors. One night I pushed her face into the floor, holding her down, trying not to break her wrist after she pulled a knife. I didn't want her cutting me. I didn't want her cutting herself. I'd only fucked up one time, when I was drunk, when I always fucked up, but she knew it would happen again just like I knew. When she found out, she opened the cabinet where I kept my whiskey and tipped a quarter bottle of Maker's into her mouth. Then she pulled a Wüsthof 5-inch serrated from the set we'd received as a wedding gift. Then she came at me. Then I pushed her face into the floor. The next day, sad and exhausted, the headache behind her eyes, my wife of one year told me she was leaving. I didn't protest. Her eyes watered and my cock went hard.

Corey's mother answered the door. It was Wednesday. She was dressed like Monday, only she wore a different T-shirt. Her husband was nowhere around. He had to be working hard. He had to be making money to keep his family happy and healthy with a floor-through apartment, a shadow therapist, a private karate instructor who didn't know karate.

She said a quick hello and turned to her son. He was standing behind her, looking at the floor. He was wearing his gi.

"You remember Marcus," she said.

He didn't say anything.

"It's 3 o'clock, Corey. It's time for your karate lesson." And she said to me but for Corey too, "Corey was practicing his karate before he went to school today."

I wanted to say something smart. About how Corey would soon be beating the shit out of his autistic classmates. About how karate would make Corey a better, more belligerent man. It was hard to tell if Corey's mother had a sense of humor.

"Wonderful," I said. It didn't sound like me. I didn't know if I'd ever said the word *wonderful* out loud.

"Can I offer you something to drink?"

"No thanks. I'll just change and we can start."

I walked down the hall. The kitchen was huge and open, a square island of granite in the center, pots and pans hanging off a rack above, a state-of-the-art oven with six gas burners and a refrigerator that looked display-worthy at the Museum of Design. I passed two closed doors, probably guest bedrooms. The third door was open, the guest bathroom. I went in, closed the door, unzipped my gym bag, changed from my clothes to my once-used gi. Tightened my fake black belt. Took a leak. Checked my face in the mirror. My eyes were puffy from too much alcohol. It was a beautiful bathroom. There was a bowl of fresh lemons on the toilet top.

The boy was waiting for me in the studio. The shadow therapist was sitting on her chair in the corner watching him. In the mirror
I could see her back, the back of her neck, the back of her head. She
looked uncomfortable. She wasn't talking to the kid or joking around
with him. He was looking at the floor.

"I hear you were practicing your karate moves, Corey-san?" I
said.

Corey didn't say anything.

"Well, that's what I heard. Practice makes perfect, so you're
doing the right thing. The more you practice, the easier it gets. And
once you perfect one move, we can work on the next move and the
next. Let's do our stretches first."

We stretched our legs. We stretched our arms, circling them in
the air. We stretched our backs. I didn't look at the shadow therapist
looking at us. I wondered if she was there to protect the kid from tan-
trums or outbursts, or if she was there to make sure I wasn't some child
molester. I always felt a little strange around kids. There was so much
awareness, so much over-protection, that an unattached man talking
to a kid seemed like a crime. It had to be good for the karate-teaching
business. With all those creeps out there, someone needed to teach kids
how to kick some ass.

I went to bars. I drank until the warm feeling came over me,
and I drank more. When I woke, usually in the early afternoon, I tried
to connect the missing pieces of the night.

Corey answered the door. He was looking down at a place
between my Nikes. Then he stepped backward from the door, four even
steps, turned around, and walked down the hall.

I changed.

The dance studio where we worked out didn't smell like working out. It didn't even smell like play. It was spotless, cleaned daily, I assumed, by a maid, not a speck of dust on the floor, not a single smudge on the mirrored walls. Corey never looked at himself in the mirrors. He kept his head down.

He had his routines. I had my routines. I'd change into my gi in the bathroom. I'd take a leak. I'd check how much damage my drinking had done to my eyes. I'd walk toward Corey, extra heavy on my feet so he'd hear me, so he'd know we were ready to begin. I'd say, Good afternoon, Corey-san. He wouldn't say anything. I'd say, Let's start with stretching, Corey-san. I'd stretch out my leg and he'd stretch out his leg. I'd stretch out my other leg and he'd stretch out his other leg. I'd stretch out my back and he'd do the same. He was limber for being such a tight kid. I wasn't that limber, and I wondered if the shadow noticed. She never said anything. I had several excuses ready but never had to use them. Slipped discs from full-contact sparring. Back injury from a surprise attack in the bamboo jungles outside Kyoto. When I was working with the kid, my focus really was on him and she really was a shadow, something unnoticed until I started thinking about noticing shadows.

I looked at apartments. They were all too much. I'd check out a listing, take the sheet prepared by the realtor, look at the floor plan, look at the rent, do the math. I could budget myself, limit my spending to ten dollars a day for food and expenses. I could live without cable, without Internet access. I could drink at home instead of at bars. Or I could call up my old landlord, see if he had a cell-sized studio available. I'd ask him about the wiry-haired woman. I'd ask him about the locksmith who visited the liquor store downstairs. I'd remind the landlord I had a history there. He had to have a room somewhere.

"Yes," he said.

It was the first time I'd heard the kid speak. He had a quiet voice, almost a whisper, almost a whistle in the way he said the *s* in *yes*.

"Great. Did you feel good?"

"Yes."

"Did you feel strong?"

"Yes."

I liked the way he said *yes*. I could have asked him a whole list of questions. The shadow was watching us. The kid had just kicked me. He'd lifted his leg perfectly, put his weight into the kick, and landed it perfectly, right above my black belt. It didn't wind me, but I'd definitely felt the impact.

"Okay," I said. "Again."

He lifted his leg, snapped it forward. Same place, right above the belt.

"Good?"

"Yes," he said.

"Strong?"

"Yes."

He liked repetition. Repetition was necessary to perfect the moves. He kicked me again and again. He could have kicked me straight for a full hour, past a full hour, until his mother walked in and told him it was time to go to bed. I let him kick me over and over, asking him if he felt good, asking him if he felt strong, asking him if he felt like he was ready to take his first belt test. Yes. Yes. Yes.

I packed my winter clothes into boxes. I still hadn't found a place. It was getting warmer. I could sleep outside. I could join a gym, shower there in the morning, keep some clothes in a locker. I could drink until closing time and walk to the park. With enough alcohol in my blood, I could pretend the ground was my mattress, my balled-up sweatshirt my pillow, and in Central Park the air was almost fresh.

We worked out three days a week. We'd been working out three days a week for five weeks. Sometimes, before our workout, I'd watch a martial arts video on YouTube, memorize a move to teach him. Sometimes, flipping through channels, I'd stop at a karate movie and throw kicks and punches at the men pretending.

I had one week left before the lease ran out. Less really. Six nights. I'd stopped looking for apartments. It was too depressing.

His body looked different. His arms had new muscle. His fists looked tighter, stronger. His smooth stomach looked harder, flatter. I could see the start of a six-pack, his gi revealing skin after he'd kicked and kicked, punched and punched, and his belt loosened. He still looked down, but his head was at a different angle, as if the coin he was looking for wasn't at his feet but suspended a few inches in the air. If I could raise the invisible coin to eye-level, he'd be looking straight ahead. He was a good-looking kid. He looked like his mother except for his eyes. Hers were sad and tired. His were distant. Not distant sad, just distant. He spoke more too. He said, Thank you, Marcus-san at the end of each lesson. He said, See you tomorrow, Marcus-san when he walked me to the door. His shadow therapist stood behind him and never said anything. After our last lesson, Corey had followed me out into the hall. I pressed the button for the elevator. We could hear the pulleys. The sliding metal gate.

I looked at Corey to say goodbye and there he was, looking me straight in the eyes.

"See?" I said.

He didn't say anything.

"See? It's easy. Eyes to eyes. That's better than a black belt," I said.

He held my eyes and held my eyes and I smiled. Then he moved his eyes, looked down.

"Good man," I said.

I walked into the elevator. The metal gate slid shut.

"Fast," I said.

And the doorman listened, yanked the handle hard. The drop felt good, like excitement.

She'd given me the ring. On her way out, her last possessions packed into the back seat of a friend's car, she'd stopped. In one hand, her desk lamp, electric cord trailing. In her other hand, the robin's-egg blue Tiffany box. She smiled the quiet smile I'd fallen for, fell for every time after we fought, after we made up, saying we had to stop. I'd remember my vow to be a better man and I'd try. For weeks. For days. At the end I couldn't make it stretch for a few hours. Something said, something done, I'd react, she'd react. It was all too hard. She smiled her smile, handed me the Tiffany box with the engagement ring inside. She still wore her wedding ring. I still wore mine. They were titanium, the longest-lasting metal. I took the box. I didn't ask for it. I would never have asked for it. But she knew I needed the money, that I'd spent my savings on a diamond that wasn't close to a carat but fit her thin finger perfectly. Did you look at your ring today? I'd say when we first got engaged. I looked at my ring today, she'd say.

His mother answered the door. She looked tired. She looked sad. She looked like she had something to say. Corey wasn't behind her.

"Today is bad," she said.

It was bad. It was a year ago, exactly, that I'd been married. It was a year ago that I'd made my toast to be a better man. Two days later we moved into our apartment. I picked her up and walked her through the threshold like we hadn't already been married for two days, carried her to the bedroom, put her down on the bed. The bed was gone. I was sleeping on the floor, a leaky air-mattress between body and wood.

"I would have called you earlier, but it just happened," Corey's mother said.

"What just happened?"

"He hit Dr. Parness."

"The shadow. The shadow therapist."

"Yes."

I clenched my jaw. I didn't want to laugh in front of her. And I didn't want to hear my laugh. I had a mean laugh sometimes.

"He hasn't lashed out like that for two years," she said. "He was doing so well."

"Maybe he's still doing well."

"What do you mean?"

I didn't know what I meant, not exactly, not to explain it. But then I remembered. I had a BA in Psychology. A Master's in Special Education. A successful stint at The Giving School in Seattle. I'd been living in an empty apartment for so many weeks, what I wasn't felt more comfortable than what I was.

"He's asserting himself," I said. "He's angry that he needs to be followed all the time. He's angry at the world and he's letting out his anger. If I had that woman sitting behind me or standing behind me and watching me all the time, I'd be angry too. It's not natural."

"No," she said.

"No," she said again. "It's not natural."

"You can't fault your son for lashing out sometimes."

"It's the way he does it," she said. "It's like he's possessed. It's like he can't help it only worse. It's like he'll never be able to help it, never."

"Never," I repeated. I didn't throw the punch.

"Dr. Parness is a professional. She comes highly recommended. She's been with him for eleven months. She was against these karate lessons. She predicted this would happen, but Corey kept asking about karate, over and over. That's how he does it. That's how he does everything, over and over and over and over."

She started to cry. It was the quietest crying. She put her hands to her eyes and didn't make a sound. Her wrists became wet.

"I'm sorry," she said.

She rubbed her eyes and looked at me. I had a hard-on. I shifted my gym bag.

"I'm sorry," she said again. "It's been a rough few weeks."

It wasn't just the kid. I could hear that.

"Is Dr. Parness here?"

"She left. I asked her to leave for the day. Corey is still very angry. I think you should leave too. I think it's better if he's alone."

"I've been very angry," I said.

"We've all been angry."

"But I've been very angry. I used to be very angry all the time. Then I started karate. It channeled things somehow. It didn't cure them. It didn't take all the anger away. But if it took everything away, I wouldn't trust it."

"Trust," she said. The crying, even if it was quiet, was out of her.

"He was talking to me. He was looking at me. I saw him

changing. He'll never change completely, but he changed a little."

We were standing there, she inside the doorway, me outside the doorway. I wanted to go inside. I wanted to change into my gi, tighten my belt around my waist, feel the wood floor against my feet. I wanted to stretch. I wanted to kick. I wanted to punch. And I wanted to see Corey doing what I did. He never looked in the mirror, so I could look in the mirror and see him, see us, and he never knew I was watching.

"I think you should let me come in," I said.

"No."

"Don't say no."

"He's in his room. He's grounded."

"Unground him."

Her eyes were tired.

"I think I know what I'm doing," I said.

She moved away from the door and I walked in.

I walked to the bathroom. I changed into my gi. I tightened my belt. I walked barefoot to the studio.

I took my position, legs spread, fists at my hips, ready, waiting. I heard her talking to him. I couldn't hear the words, but I could hear the tone. Sad. Tired. And patient. Over and over and over and over, she'd said.

I waited. I kept my eyes on a place in front of my feet. I didn't feel like looking in the mirror.

I heard his bare feet on the floor.

I looked up. I saw him, the reflection of him, walk into the room and take his position next to me. He spread his legs. He put his fists at his hips.

"Angry," he said. It wasn't as comforting as when he said *yes*, there was no sweet whistle at the end of the word. But the word, *angry*, wasn't as hard sounding when he said it. The way he said it, anger was just something that happened.

"What are you angry about?"

He punched the air.

You didn't have to be married and separated. You didn't have to make promises you couldn't keep. You didn't have to be desperate for money, for a place to live. You didn't need a specific reason. It could just take you over and not just because you couldn't be a better man. It was just a feeling and I'd had that feeling forever. Corey had so much coming at him he had to do things, repetitively, over and over.

"Angry," he said again and punched the air again.

I followed him. I punched the air.

We stood there punching.

Punching and punching.

And we were yelling with our punches. Not angry yells. Not desperate yells. Joyful yells. Letting-go yells. Giving in to ourselves.

picasso's model

"How long has that church's clock been stuck?"

"For as long as I've known," she says. "They try to fix it sometimes. It works for a few days and then stops."

"10:10. Like an advertisement."

I'm sitting on brownstone steps. They're not mine. Sometimes
after work, too tired to go home and crash, I buy a beer and sit outside somewhere nearby to put away my night making drinks, making
change, making small talk. Usually no one's on their steps this late, the
city's version of porch sitting, but she came out, lit a cigarette, and sat
on her brownstone steps next to me.

"Have you been inside?"

"No."

"It's a beautiful church."

"I have a friend who thinks he's found Jesus," I say. "If he was
here right now, maybe we'd go in."

"It's closed."

"That never stopped us."

"Good for you. Good for you and your friend. A couple of reb-
els. Am I safe or should I lock my door?"

"I'm staying outside."

She smiles. She takes a pull off her cigarette, lets the smoke out
slow.

"You're staying outside. Your friend who thinks he's found

Jesus isn't here. I think I'm safe."

She finishes her cigarette and puts it out on the step. She's old and slow but elegant too, her moves from a time when movies got shot in Technicolor.

"He was an actor. He was trying to make it as an actor, but I don't think he fully believed it would happen. He didn't try hard enough. I think he knew if he tried hard and it didn't happen, it would have been too much. He's moved from Hollywood dreams to Jesus and he says he believes, but every now and then the words slip out. Make it. The way he says it still sounds like one word. Makeit. I think Hollywood's still in him."

"Artistic dreams. They're hard to break."

"Make it, making it, the word or words sound like they're close to an end point, but there's really no end to making it. It's a false promise. He still doesn't recognize that part and I've never told him."

"Tell him."

"He's in California."

"You can still tell him."

She takes another cigarette from her pack. She offers me one. I take it. She lights mine. She lights hers.

"Thank you."

"You're welcome."

"There's a movie line from *Easy Rider*. If I told him, I'd tell him that line. He knows the scene. He knows the line, but I'd still tell him."

"Tell me."

I take another pull. The smoke pushes the beer, moves me off center, a good feeling. I blur my eyes and make the streetlights open to halos.

"The two bikers, the main characters, they're not just bikers.

They're drug runners. They're drug users too, they love the serenity of drugs and the high, but they're drug runners first, that's what they do and how they make their money. Near the end of the movie, before the violence of their work catches up with them, they're in a graveyard and one of them, the one called Captain America, says the line. *We blew it.* All that living in the moment and driving America's highways and acting free is just pretend or has pretend attached to it. They've had other motives all along, the whole movie, and Captain America finally admits it. They're stuck. They realize too late the way they've lived isn't pure, and they're never able to drive away from that. They're killed in the next scene. Their light, whatever light they felt getting high and riding their bikes and even pretending they were free, that light goes out. Their dream isn't their end point. Their violent death is. I still want to live like a movie sometimes, but I'm aware of it. It happens enough, that movie feeling, where it's enough or almost enough. For my friend it still isn't. Or wasn't. I think he's still stuck. Maybe I don't know him well enough anymore to know."

"Maybe you don't."

"He grew up rough. Maybe that's part of why he can't admit some things. Maybe that's why the word Makeit still slips out sometimes. But that's too easy."

"*Easy Rider,*" she says.

"It's a good movie. It doesn't have an easy backstory. There's no A equals B. Those are the movies I like best. The ones closer to life where the in-between doesn't add up so neatly."

She inhales long and slow and holds the smoke longer than seems possible.

"There can be a whole lifetime between A and B. What happens later is always tied to something earlier," she says, and the smoke comes out. "Especially at the end."

"Tied to and equal aren't the same."

"There's always that connecting string. It's more of a bass string than a violin's. Those lower notes stick."

We finish our cigarettes. We put them out on the steps. There's no one on the street. My shift at the bar feels almost out of me. I'll walk back to my apartment and shower and sleep late.

"Do you like Picasso?" she says.

"I do. I've looked at some of his paintings for a long time. I do that when I want something to stay with me."

"Picasso's models are defined by Picasso, which is a kind of pretend. There's so much of him in them, they aren't fully themselves."

"Good thing I never stood for Picasso."

"If you had you'd be immortal."

"If I had I'd be very old."

"Have you stood for artists?"

"I have."

"I can see that. You have good lines."

"Are you an artist?"

"More of a pretend one," she says.

"With him," she says, "with Picasso, your eyes would be there, and your mouth would be there." She smiles.

She looks across the street, maybe at the clock.

"I once had dinner with one of his models," she says. "It was a dinner party and she was still very beautiful as an old woman. She was with a young man, who looked like a gigolo. There were a number of guests, very successful people from different fields and a few artists I knew, but she was the one everyone paid attention to the whole evening. It felt like we were sitting with a disciple. Picasso's model. I remember feeling, and I remember others saying after, that it felt like we were sitting with a part of him too. She was famous because of him. She was rich because of him. He gave her several of his paintings and drawings and whenever she needed money, she sold one off. What she'd done for him had been many decades before, but he was still at the forefront of everything she was. She mentioned that singular fact during dinner, that she had modeled for Picasso, as I'm sure she mentioned her connection to Picasso at every dinner, or waited for someone to mention it, and when she left the dinner party, that's all we talked about, the residue of Picasso still in her chair."

half a dead man

The utility phone goes off, two loud buzzes, too early on Saturday morning. My girlfriend had a long week at work so the call wakes her, but I'm up anyway, thinking, and I get out of bed, answer the phone, find out Curt's in the lobby. I tell the doorman I'll be right down. I put on sweats, grab my wallet since money will probably be involved. I know the doorman's watching me on the monitor while I tie my sneakers in the elevator, but when I get to the lobby the doorman's watching Curt and for good reason. Curt looks wrecked. His hair is disheveled, his clothes are stained with flashing tar and aluminum coating, and as I walk the long walk across freshly waxed tiles I see red explosions in his eyes.

"You're not going to believe it," Curt says.

I'm sure I will. Curt lives an edgy life romanticized by movies that in real life isn't romantic at all. His filthy clothes are real. His stale breath is real. His hacking cough is real from at least a pack a day, the pack of Marlboros tucked under the short sleeve of his T-shirt. I'd bummed cigarettes off him until I started buying packs myself. That was years ago. Years ago I'd lived near the edge too, but the air-conditioned lobby of a luxury building is something I'm used to now, like having a doorman, like fine dining in trendy restaurants, drinking martinis instead of vodka straight from the bottle.

"What happened?" I say.

"I'm done."

And Curt gives me the rundown of the damage. He's been

evicted from his apartment. He's been living out of his truck for the past four days. He's broke. He finished up a 24-hour coke binge two days ago and hasn't slept since Tuesday. He's a great story teller and I see it all: the marshals knocking on his door, showing no mercy, giving him fifteen minutes to clear out whatever stuff he can, slapping on the padlock, and, when the marshals leave, Curt leaning against his truck, surveying his possessions stacked on the sidewalk, while people stop to ask if he's selling his TV, his computer, his photograph of Marlon Brando on a motorcycle, leather cap cocked over sunlight-squinted eyes.

"I need a shower," Curt says. "I could use some money if you can loan me some."

The doorman's watching us, so I lower my voice. "What do you want to do first?"

"I stink like a homeless man," Curt says.

"Let's go up."

We take the elevator and before I open our padlock-free door I tell Curt to keep it down, Jenny's still sleeping. Jenny has met Curt a couple of times. She knows he's an old friend. She knows we met in an acting class. We've run into Curt in the neighborhood, usually around Washington Square, and the three of us even went out to eat once. Jenny still jokes about the extra mayonnaise Curt put on his cheeseburger, a throwback order to when clogged arteries weren't considered. Jenny works out with a personal trainer three times a week and runs the New York City Marathon every fall and I've started running because of her. At first I couldn't make it around the block, my lungs raw from too many cigarettes, my liver sore from too much straight alcohol, but now I do four miles at a pop, time myself on the last mile. I've started breaking seven minutes.

Curt's eyes take in Jenny's place. A two-level apartment in the city is something to behold, especially after sleeping four nights in a pickup truck. I get a clean towel from the linen closet, the towels neatly folded and stacked, not by me, and point Curt to the guest bathroom.

"Do you have a razor?" Curt says. "I could use a shave."

"I'll get you one."

"I'm going to shave all my pubes and my asshole. I'm going to make myself into the boy I am."

Jenny's upstairs sleeping, but I start laughing, loud, and Curt starts laughing loud. When he first came to New York, came back to New York after ten years away, the two of us picked up where we'd left off. We went out drinking, caused some trouble, stayed outside when the weather got nice. We played a lot of tennis on the Riverside courts without ever getting permits. Sometimes we'd join a softball game in Central Park, try to hit line drives at the people sitting in the stands cheering for their friends, not us, two strangers to the team. Then Curt's roof repair business got busy and he spent his days stopping leaks from Connecticut to New Jersey, a one-man, one-cellphone, truck-and-ladder operation.

"Anything else?" I say.

"I need some socks."

Curt goes into the bathroom. I go upstairs. Jenny has her eyes open.

"What's going on?" she says.

"Curt got kicked out of his place. The marshals came and padlocked his door."

"You knew that was coming."

"That doesn't make it easier."

"He should have looked for another place months ago," Jenny says, pulling the duvet to her chin. "He's been living over his head for months."

"He thought his business would recover."

Downstairs the water comes on. If Jenny weren't here, Curt would be belting out show tunes with made-up lyrics about failure, or throwing exaggerated kicks and punches at the shower curtain, making ninja noises, pretending to beat himself down.

"He's been thinking that for a year," she says.

"I thought it too. It's not like there's a shortage of roofs in this city."

"Most businesses fail. It's not that easy."

"Obviously."

"Obviously," she repeats.

"Christ. I'm sorry he woke you. The guy's been homeless for four days."

I take a pair of clean socks from my drawer, just laundered by the once-a-week cleaning woman, get a new razor from the upstairs bathroom, and go downstairs. The duplex is Jenny's. She works in the financial district for a small investment bank. When we met, I never would have guessed she was a Wall Street type. She was the best dancer on the floor, and when she ordered her Johnny Walker Black neat, the bartender had smiled and nodded his head. I'd been that bartender.

I put the razor on the sink, the socks on top of Curt's dirty clothes piled on the closed toilet seat. He opens the shower curtain with his balls lathered up, pretending to jerk off.

"Sorry," he says. "I thought you were upstairs. You want to hand me that razor?"

"No."

"Is she upset?"

"She's not thrilled."

"Don't worry. I'll take you out for breakfast and you'll forget all your problems. Steak and eggs. Side order of French toast. My treat. I'll let you run first."

Curt closes the shower curtain. Coughs. Spits. Coughs again. I walk into the living room, lift the shade to look outside, and it's perfect timing. The Queen Mary 2 moves by, massive, slow motion, an even tail of whitewash behind, the Statue of Liberty in the background. Rows of miniature people stand on deck looking at New York. I watch the boat until it's near the mouth of the harbor. I put my back against the Persian rug and start doing crunches.

Showered, shaved, his hair brushed back wet, Curt is good looking again. There's still a smudge of tar on his forearms, making his blond hairs stiff and black, that would probably be there even if he hadn't been evicted. The materials he works with stick around. Curt sits on the couch and leans his head all the way back.

"If I closed my eyes, I could sleep twenty hours straight."

"What are you going to do?"

"This city," Curt says. "I park on these quiet side streets and every few hours a cop will knock on my window and wake me up. I was on Leroy Street last night. Ask anyone where Leroy Street is and I bet ninety percent of New Yorkers wouldn't know it existed, but the cops sure do. One cop cuffed me. He ran my license and they've still got me down for an old warrant. It's been ten years. I told the cop it was ten years and the statute of limitations ran out. He had to call his sergeant before he took the cuffs off."

"What are you going to do?"

"I thought Jenny could get a hotel room and you and me could live here for the rest of our lives."

"I'll go up and tell her."

"I'll keep sleeping in my truck," Curt says. "My phone's still on. They didn't disconnect my number yet. I have a fifteen-thousand-dollar job that could break any minute."

I've heard about these any-minute job breaks before. I don't say anything, keep doing crunches, straining my stomach muscles, not letting myself breathe hard, not letting Curt see I'm tired.

"As soon as that big aluminum-coat job fell through, it all changed," Curt says. "I had eighty-thousand dollars of estimates out and none of them went. Not a single one. I'm not going back to California."

"What about finding a cheap place in Connecticut? Some of your business is there."

"If I leave Manhattan, I'll go crazy. I missed this place for ten years. I don't want to miss it for ten more. I should kill that property manager who canceled the job. Semenov. I should throw that little Russian fucker off the roof. Fucking Semenov. He started my bad luck."

I do a final crunch and sit up.

"Twenty," Curt says.

"Try three hundred."

"I counted twenty."

He balls himself into the fetal position and tucks one of Jenny's decorative pillows under his head.

"This is the most comfortable couch I've ever sat on."

"Let's hit the bank," I say.

"Bad news every day," Curt says. "I'm on the low swing. What about you? You must be on the upswing if I'm down."

"That's the way it goes with us."

"A couple more days of homelessness and your book will get taken."

"It was taken a week ago."

"No."

"It was."

Curt sits up. He crosses his eyes and opens his mouth like he's just taken a bullet to the back of his head.

"Hold on," Curt says. "Hold on. Easy. Easy. Breathe out. Nice and easy. Okay."

He uncrosses his eyes.

"I'm taking off from work," I say. "I need to revise and edit and do some work in the digital lab at ICP."

"The photography place. You think I could sleep there?"

"Sure."

"Sorry. Congratulations. That's great. You did it. You made it. They're going to publish your book."

My collection of stories with accompanying photographs is about subway tragedies. I have a contact at the Transit Authority and he calls me whenever someone's pushed onto the tracks, slashed in a station, found dead in a car. My last good photograph, the last photograph that inspired a story, I took on the D Train. It's a series of a man who looks like he's sleeping, only his face is white and there's no air going into or out of his lungs. He must have closed his eyes and died. I never found out how many times he traveled back and forth, uptown and downtown, before someone realized the man was dead. I focused on his thick hands, gray hairs above the knuckles, still holding a plastic bag. Through the plastic there's a six-pack of Coke and a box of Wheaties.

Curt gets off the couch, readjusts the pack of Marlboros under his sleeve. His sneakers are streaked with flashing tar. When we first met, he needed a new pair of sneakers. He opted for gray ones so they wouldn't look dirty too quickly. That's how I knew he'd grown up poor. We walk out of Jenny's apartment, take the elevator down, walk past the doorman, out to the street.

"You like that guy watching your every move?"

"I don't," I say.

"I couldn't take it. What happens if you're drunk?"

"I concentrate on walking straight and saying good evening without slurring."

"This chick that sold me the crack keeps the vials under her gums. Instead of chewing tobacco, she has a mouthful of rocks. It's really kind of cool watching her take them out."

"You're not using this money for drugs."

"I needed a night to let loose after I got evicted. You know how it is. Should we take my truck?"

"Let's walk."

We pass the flower shops, the coffeehouses with trays of muffins in the windows, the high-end clothing stores. The bank is near the subway entrance, Christopher Street, the number 1 local. Five years ago, I photographed a gay man beaten in this station. He was lying against the turnstile, his lips cut and swollen like his mouth had burst, his nose turning purple and pointing to the side. I'd spent many hours working on the shots. I wanted the shadows of the turnstile to hold the same slick feel as the blood on his face. The story I wrote wasn't about the beaten man. It was about a man taking the subway who never noticed the beaten man. He was going downtown to break up with his girlfriend and he was feeling, or thought he was feeling, alive. When I couldn't find a publisher for my story collection, when I couldn't even find an agent to get my manuscript to the right editor, I started craving success more than the work. I needed a book. There was no point doing new work if my old work didn't sell. I'd heard the Van Gogh story too many times. The great master never sold his paintings while living but perfected his craft anyway and achieved immortality after he died. Artists never recounted that story, not real artists, only non-artists and dabblers. Fame before death was what I wanted. I hadn't written a new story or taken a good photograph in years, but I'd sold a book.

"How much?" I say.

"I need about six hundred. Five would be great. I could use six."

Curt waits outside. I slip in my card, withdraw six hundred for Curt, fifty for me, crisp twenties and a beat-up ten. I hand Curt the money and he thanks me, puts the bills in his pocket, finishes his cigarette, presses it cold with his foot.

"I'll get this back to you," he says. "That fifteen-thousand-dollar job could break today. You want to get some breakfast? I'll take you out for breakfast."

"You'll take me out?"

"I'll pay it all back. This six hundred and the other eight hundred. I'll take it right off the top of my next job."

"I know you will."

He looks past me. He looks down. He rubs his thumb over the tar smudge on his forearm.

"There's no one else I could ask," he says. "My mom's tapped out and I'm not talking to my brother."

"Let's visit the Carnegie. See if they give us another free meal."

We go underground. No one's in the station. The next train arrives in 2 minutes. The time is 6:15. I'm not even sure the Carnegie is open, famous for its ridiculously oversized sandwiches, famous for us as the easiest place to eat and run. I tap my card for Curt, then me. I walk to the edge of the platform and look into the darkness. When I first moved to the city, I looked in and saw a severed body. Top half. Torso, arms, head. I always carried a point and shoot camera and took the shots before I told the station attendant there was half a dead man on the tracks. That was how I found my subject.

"I hope Jenny isn't too pissed," Curt says. "I didn't realize it was so early."

"I was up."

"I keep waking at dawn. As soon as the sun hits my mirrors. I must never be that asleep."

"Rise and shine."

I feel the vibration of the train, see the front lights, wait for the cars to slow and stop. The last car's almost empty. The doors open. We go in and sit down. The air conditioning smells stale.

"New York, New York," Curt says like it's a wall.

"I'm bored," I say. "Bored of this city."

"Where would you go?"

"I don't know. I get stir crazy any time I'm somewhere else. Paris was good. Rome. Berlin. New York has the numbers and the anonymity and the speed. Sometimes I get tired of it. I don't know where I'd go."

"I wish I was bored," Curt says. "I'm constantly going over my expenses in my head. 1,600 for truck insurance, 80 for phone, I owe 3,400 on my credit card, 7,500 on back rent. I have the tax people calling me up for an interview. Let's move in together. Seriously. If we split the rent, we could afford to live in a decent place."

"I live in a decent place."

"I've got to meet a rich girl. I used to meet all kinds of rich girls."

"If they arrest you for tax fraud, you'll live rent free."

"I wouldn't care right now."

The train slows and stops. The doors open. No one comes in. The doors close. The train moves.

"You did it," Curt says. "You got your book taken."

"It hasn't sunk in yet," I say.

"Too many years of hurt for it to heal that quickly, right? I know."

"I want to see my book on the shelves."

I grab the cross bar above and lift myself up. I do a set of twenty pull-ups, don't let myself breathe hard. Aware. Always aware. My camera pointed at me. At the end of the car, a real homeless man, who hasn't showered, who hasn't borrowed money, who holds a garbage bag full of cans, smiles a lunatic smile.

"Three," Curt says.

"Twenty."

"What does this mean for you?" Curt says. "What kind of fame are we talking about?"

"I'm still taking subways."

"Women are going to love it when you tell them you've got a book."

"I haven't told anyone yet."

"You will."

"When I sign the contract, I will."

"A contract. Shit. This is real."

I look at our reflections in the subway window. Blurred from the unwashed glass and the speed and the dark tunnel it could be ten years ago.

"Remember that guy we served last winter?" Curt says. "I was listening to the tape we made in the truck."

Curt and I had served fake papers to a property manager who owed Curt money. He'd never seen Curt, so Curt and I dressed like undercover officers, tinted sunglasses and matching dark windbreakers. While I served the guy papers, Curt wandered around the office with his phone in his pocket, playing our recording of made-up walkie-talkie sounds and codes. A 15-40 on Ninth Street. A stolen 23-20 recovered on the corner of Varick. A 454 APB for all units. The static sounded real and the property manager immediately wrote out a check to Curt's business. I'd taken a photograph of Curt as an undercover officer, my image reflected in his tinted shades. Curt had it framed and hanging in his bedroom when he'd had a bedroom.

"We've done it all," Curt says. "Now you have a book contract."

"I'm done."

"Could you die right now? If you died right now, would you feel complete?"

"Not yet."

"I've been thinking of calling it a day," Curt says.

"And do what? Aluminum-coat yourself and jump off the roof?"

"Something like that."

"Your business can still take off. Your overhead was too high. You were renting an apartment you couldn't afford."

"I can't afford any place in the city. Come on. Why don't you move out of Jenny's apartment and we'll look for a place?"

"I don't know."

We ride on, sitting next to each other, our sneakers practically touching, mine new and white and Curt's streaked with tar, once white, now closer to gray. We get off at 50th Street and walk uptown. The streets around Rockefeller Center are busy on weekdays, but this morning they're quiet. A street-sweeping truck moves along the avenue, making a wet swath that ends at the curb.

The Carnegie Deli is open and crowded. Tourists. Early risers. College kids feeding their hangovers meat and grease. The hostess calls out Two to a waiter in back, walks us to our table, hands us oversized menus. Everything's too big here. The menus. The sandwiches. The giant cheesecakes circulating in the display case. Even the strawberries on top are huge.

"You recognize him?" Curt says.

"He waited on us one time. Not the last time."

Our one-time waiter takes our order. We both get lox, eggs and onions, and chocolate malteds. Curt orders an extra plate of home fries and a side of French toast. The gluttonous order guarantees we'll run. The last time we were here we'd come from Central Park. We'd each lined a foul ball into the bleachers and my shot ricocheted off a man's arm, leaving a welt the literal size of a softball. We'd kept our Yankees caps on in the Carnegie, and before we ordered too much food, we pulled the brims low over our heads. All the waiter saw were two caps and two mouths. No eyes. No noses. Nothing but mouths ordering food to devour. That waiter had been too old for the job. I pictured varicose veins under his black pants, misshapen toes from too many hours on his feet, a back broken from carrying plates piled high with deli meats and cheeses. We ate, left a tip, and ran.

"I love their French toast," Curt says.

"Are you in good enough shape?"

"I may look like shit, but I can still move. Do you think he recognizes us?"

"Definitely. The French toast reminded him."

"Game on."

The couple at the next table are tourists. Their clothes are slightly off. Their too-open eyes survey the celebrity photographs that cover the Carnegie's walls. They nod politely at us.

"You read about this place, right?" Curt says.

"As a matter of fact, we did," the man says. "According to the guide, it's the best deli in all New York City."

Curt flashes a smile that's not real. It's worse when the woman smiles back, happy to make a connection on their travels.

"Are you from here?" she says.

"Born and bred," Curt says. "No place like it."

"It's certainly impressive."

"That's the most impressive thing about it," Curt says.

The woman's smile flattens, not sure if he's serious or joking.

"What do you two do here?" she asks.

"I'm a lawyer and my friend is a famous photographer. He's taken many of the pictures you see on the walls."

"Is that right?" the man says.

"I did," I say. "It's a good way to meet famous people."

"Who's the most famous person you ever photographed?" the woman says.

"Are we talking politics, sports, or creative geniuses?"

"Anything, I guess."

"He once photographed Marlon Brando," Curt says. "His picture's on the wall somewhere around here. That's why we get to eat for free."

"Lucky you," the woman says.

"I'm an entertainment lawyer," Curt says.

If he'd grown up in a different kind of home, if he'd finished high school and gone to college, if he'd seen another world at a younger age, he could have been anything. He never used his past as an excuse, but his stories were brutal. Curt washing pots in a restaurant at ten years old, twenty hours on weekends, to help pay rent. Curt watching his mother swing a baseball bat into his drunk father's knee. Curt telling his father to remove his glasses before Curt knocked him out. That was the day Curt left home and moved to New York the first time. He'd told me each story once, vividly, like a print he'd worked on for a long time.

The waiter sets down two large plates and we turn from our city's guests to our eggs. We're halfway done when the French toast arrives. Curt smothers the slices in butter and syrup and cuts them into chunks.

"Dig in," he says.

We eat quickly. Whenever it's sure we'll run, we never fully enjoy the meal. The getting away is what we're looking toward, so the meal's just prologue, something to skim through before the real story begins. We also don't trust each other. I've made several quick exits while Curt was in the middle of chewing an expensive piece of steak, and Curt's excused himself many times to go to the bathroom never to return, leaving me at the table, waitstaff eying me, one diner where there'd just been two, pretending casual, waiting for the right time to run. This morning I know I'm safe. He owes me. And if he walks out first, I'll pay. I don't want to jinx my book deal. Curt's phone goes off. I've been thinking book, so it can't be good. Curt takes his phone from his pocket.

"It's Stillman," Curt says. "The fifteen-thousand-dollar job. This could be it."

Curt answers the call, starts nodding his head, the tone of his Yes, Yes, Yes not affirmative at all. Curt says something about the sealant on the roof, how he couldn't find the hole, how it was like looking for a pinprick in a parachute, how he fixed all their other roofs but this one's impossible, it's not like he hasn't tried. His eyes dull as he talks. His jaw tightens. I've seen him get this way before he starts throwing punches, but the arm holding the phone looks tired, tar-smudged, aluminum-spotted.

"Fair enough," Curt says into the phone. "You know my warranty on the last job I did for you? Forget it. It just ran out. You can fix your own fucking leaks."

Curt puts his phone on the table.

"That's all folks," Curt says.

Curt can do a good Porky Pig, can imitate that cartoon stutter before delivering the line. This time he doesn't bother. He just says the line.

Our waiter serves the out-of-town couple heaping pastrami sandwiches. They hardly notice, too busy trying to figure out why an entertainment lawyer is talking about fucking leaks and warranties. Curt forks the last piece of French toast, chews, swallows.

"Guess what?" Curt says.

"Sorry."

"It really was like looking for a pinprick."

"I believe you. I know you do good work."

"I fixed every one of his roofs. Every time there was a leak I was there."

Anything I say will sound pitying, so I keep quiet. I look at the plate where the French toast was. Melted butter stains the syrup.

"You ready?" he says.

"You should get the check first."

"I don't need the check. We've perfected this game."

"We're out of practice. It's been six months."

"Eight months," Curt says. "Eight months since our last run. I guess we've both been busy. I was thinking this morning how I've been back in New York for four whole years. If you hadn't been here, I wouldn't have lasted this long. We've had some good times."

"We're still having good times."

"Will you marry her?"

"Get the check. He's watching us."

"I don't need it. It's like riding a bike. Meet me on the corner."

I look at Curt. He looks at me. He really is my closest friend, even if we do sit on a seesaw of luck. He nods his head and his eyes sharpen. I stand and walk past the other tables, past the men slicing meats and cutting sandwiches in half. I stop at the cash register to take a toothpick so I can watch Curt standing up. He makes it look like he has all the time in the world. I turn and walk out the door and keep walking and hear the door open, hear his steps, heavy and fast, Curt behind me and next to me, the shouts of the waiter behind us, and we run.

We don't stop until we're four blocks south of the famous Carnegie Deli. We're laughing. Curt is coughing.

We walk to the subway on 50th and down the steps. It's still early. No one's around.

"He knew," Curt says.

"He remembered."

"We're memorable," Curt says.

I tap my card for Curt, then me. I don't tell him I'm not memorable yet. Not the way I want to be. I don't tell him I'm out of practice. Sending emails, making phone calls, mingling at parties, making contacts is all I do. If my book hits, I'll try to write another but don't know if I can. It's too hot underground. I look into the tunnel. No bodies.

"I guess I'll sell the truck," Curt says.

"You still have a chance."

"Do you have your camera on you?"

"I always have a camera. Point and shoot."

"Always ready. That's what I like about you. I'm not good with back-up plans."

"What does that mean?"

"She's insurance."

"I don't need insurance. I got a book."

"You do."

I hear the vibration of a train. I look in the tunnel and the darkness lightens. I step back, more concerned with my mortality in the last week, and turn to Curt. He looks at me and there's something in his eyes, maybe disappointment, maybe worry, and he jumps onto the tracks.

"Which rail is it that electrocutes you?" he yells.

He's staring at his feet.

"Get up here," I say.

"The third rail, right? If I put my foot on the third rail, I'll get zapped. Either that or the train gets me. Which should I choose?"

"Get up here, Curt."

The vibration gets louder.

"For your book, which would make the better shot?"

"Get up here," I scream.

"Get your camera out," Curt yells.

The vibration's too loud. The tunnel's filled with subway car. I'm screaming at Curt to stop. Screaming at the conductor to stop. The train passes at full speed, slows, stops. I press down the puke in my throat. The doors open. A few people get off. The doors close. The train starts. I force myself to look.

There's nothing.

Just empty track.

Curt peeks out from behind a girder. He looks at me, starts laughing.

"I had you," he says.

I don't let myself breathe hard.

"I had you," he says. "Like when we first met. I could always get one over on you back then."

Curt walks across the rails and pulls himself onto the platform. He coughs from the effort, spits on the tracks.

"I'll miss this place," he says.

Jenny has already planned the book party. Her rich friends will be there, and they'll buy the book, ask me to sign it, no longer look at me like I'm just another starving artist. I'll drink champagne and when they ask what I'm working on next I'll smile mysteriously, keep it vague.

The train's vibration diminishes. The tunnel is back to dark. I don't let myself breathe hard, try to show Curt I knew he was fucking around, try to fool myself everything is fine.

romance of the seas

You're in a Red Lobster. You've never been to a Red Lobster before, but you're here now. In fact, this wasn't your first dining choice. You checked into the hotel and drove along the usual strip and pulled into a Bennigan's. You'd never been to a Bennigan's either, but when you opened the door a waiter was bringing food back to the kitchen. You knew that wasn't a good sign.

So you turned around and walked across the parking lot to your rental. You'd been driving all day. You'd been driving for a reason. But in Charlotte, two people came. In Cincinnati, no one came. You sold two books anyway. One to the bookstore manager and one to an insane woman who said she used to work in the store's café. Her hair was chopped. She had lipstick on the tip of her nose. She'd seen the poster with your picture on it and showed up, between appointments she said, to hear you read from your novel. With two people standing there you didn't read anything. You didn't even crack the book's spine. What you did was nod your head politely as the insane woman, who might have once worked in the bookstore's café, told you about her own writing project, a story set on a dwarf planet with red grass and creatures that communicated with their taste buds. After you signed her book, she clutched it in her fingers, cuticles picked and bloody. You left the store before she had a chance to attempt taste-bud communication. You drove from Cincinnati to just outside Chicago where the hotels are cheaper, the suburbs the best place to stay for a failing writer on the road.

So now you're in a Red Lobster. You're sitting at the bar waiting for your name to be called so they can take you to a table for one. You've been calculating: For every two hundred miles driven you've sold a book and for every book sold you've made about two bucks. If you were relying on book sales to make next month's rent, you'd have to drive to that fictional planet with red grass and back again.

You drink your beer. It's a Bass Ale served in a frosted mug. You're thinking how this beer in this frosted mug is the best part of your day so far. You're looking forward to a meal that has to be better than the burgers you've been eating at rest stops along the way. You look at the restaurant's décor. There are planks with names on them, red letters stamped on driftwood-colored backgrounds. You assume this is Red Lobster's attempt to conjure up visions of old ships. One plank says *Windward Phantom*. One says *Romance of the Seas*. Your road trip was supposed to be romantic. Your readings were supposed to be events, attractive groupies showing up, expensive dinners with cutting-edge people in every city, crowds standing in line to get their books autographed. You order another beer from the bartender.

The hostess calls your name. They announce your name in each bookstore, over the loudspeaker, but the people looking over the shelves don't even glance up. Maybe you should start confronting them, tell them you've driven many miles to their pitiful cities to read from your work. The hardest thing is to see the titles they're looking at. How-to books. Self-help books. Books about cats. One guy was looking at a picture book of cranes, cranes that lift pieces of concrete. To him, a cinder block was far more interesting than your reading. You pictured operating one of those cranes, lifting the man up and up by his overalls, and swinging him into the table that displayed your unsold books.

The hostess calls your name again. You pick up your beer in its frosted mug now less frosted and walk to the woman holding the plastic menu. She takes you to a corner table. You sit, back to the wall, and survey the eaters. They grow them big in this part of the country. A man chews on the tail of a lobster, the tail too red, drawn butter dripping down his chin, his mouth working slow and steady. A woman pours salt over her mozzarella sticks. At one table three blond boys eat fish and chips swimming in tartar sauce. They already have the hangdog look of overweight men.

Your waitress comes over. She's not fat at all. She's skinny. Her hair's cut short. Her mouth's almost a frown. She looks like the kind of girl who hangs out on East Village sidewalks, showing off her piercings and tattoos, asking for money like it's a game, pretending her lack of ambition is identity enough. She isn't like that. She's working. There's sweat on her forehead. She's holding a tray full of bussed plates and empty glasses. She says she'll be back to take your order in one minute. Her voice is friendly. You tell her you're in no rush. You watch her walk away, waitress-quick and gymnast-cute. You've slept with four women on the trip so far and figure an even five will be perfect.

You look over the menu. Lobster. Shrimp. Clams. A steak for meat eaters. You decide on the butterfly shrimp. There are two prices for butterfly shrimp. There's the regular order and the captain's order, where for five bucks extra you get an added dozen shrimp. You've eaten enough on this trip. You don't need a captain's order. The salad and baked potato that come with the meal will fill you up. The waitress returns faster than you expected and sets a basket of biscuits in front of you. She asks what you'd like. You say the butterfly shrimp. She asks if you'd like the captain's order and her eyes are clear, so clear they almost sparkle, the stuff of youth, and in the mirror your eyes have been looking red and beaten at the end of each day. The waitress waits, pad poised, and you want this girl to know you're still a young man, younger than your eyes, vibrant and healthy and hearty. You say you'll have the captain's order. You smile like you're the kind of man that only orders captain's orders and still has abdominals hard as gangplanks. She asks if you'd like another beer and, hoisting your glass, you say you'll have another. She asks what kind you're drinking and you say Bass. You smile and stay on her eyes until she looks away. She flushes a little. You can tell she likes you, red eyes and all.

You finish your beer. You lean back in your chair. You look around the Red Lobster. You're thinking you could be in New York right now, leaving your little studio apartment after a day of writing, and rewarding yourself with dinner at a restaurant that doesn't feature captain's portions. You're thinking the road is just that, a road. One long road that goes on and on and looks the same everywhere and in the large scheme of things your little writings in Manhattan don't mean much to anyone, certainly not to these people in the Red Lobster. You take a postcard from your pocket, a reprint of your book cover, one of a thousand you ordered to spread the word about your first novel, and look at it. Lately you've been placing these postcards above urinals at eye level. Advertisements for yourself for a captive audience, dick in hand.

You break off a piece of biscuit. It's more lard than flour. You push the basket away and wait for your meal. You're thinking about the woman you slept with in Ann Arbor. You met her in a bar. You told her you were from New York City. You told her you were a writer. You told her you were a part-time teacher. You waited for her to ask what grade so you could say College. You disgust yourself. You took her back to the Motel 6 and woke up the next morning with a dry mouth, a head-ache from too much bourbon, and a woman puking in the bathroom.

Your waitress returns. She puts down your beer and your order and tells you to be careful of the hot plate. You tell her you're always careful, especially of plates. She smiles. You ask how her night is going. She says she's been busy. You ask if she's a student, a way to start things off. She says she wants to go back to school, but in the meantime she likes her job. You say a quizzical Really. She says she likes meeting the different people, and you look around the restaurant. You say you're from New York City. You hold her eyes. She smiles shy and looks away. She asks if you need anything else. You tell her you're fine, leaving the obvious line alone.

You watch her walk to the kitchen. You put the napkin on your lap and fork your first shrimp. You dip it into cocktail sauce, put it in your mouth, and taste the grease. There's nothing butterflied about the shrimp except its shape, nothing light or pretty. You fork another, dip, the bigshot captain hoisting his abundant catch. The two kids have finished their fish and chips and they're eyeing your shrimp. When their parents aren't looking, you open your mouth, show them your chewed food. The kids don't know what to do with that, an adult trying to gross them out, so they look away.

You have no joy. You've read the hardest thing to write is joy. You've written a few joyful moments, not many. Lately, the hardest thing to feel is joy. You can't remember the last time you felt seriously joyful. Maybe when you got your book accepted. You haven't found joy on the road. What joy is there in showing up to a city alone, looking at the buildings, passing the people, seeing the sights like a checklist with no one to share them with? Part of the romance of the road, of the true on-the-road experience, is to be on your own, but it's also very depressing. It's not the actual driving. The driving is fine. You have the feel of the car and the wheel in your hands. You can speed and pass and weave. You can play games with other drivers, dare them to pass you, accelerate just enough when they go by that they have to accelerate more, more than they want, more than they should, and sometimes a cop nails them just at that moment. You lift your hand, wave, let them know the king of the road is sometimes the slower man. You drive and you get to your destination and you walk around and there's nothing to do except drink, kill time, flirt with a stranger, wait until you need to show up at the bookstore so you can read a few pages to a few people and sign a few books and then, thank goodness, get in the car and drive.

You're halfway through the butterfly shrimp. You're almost done with your third beer. You're feeling buzzed, but not so buzzed you can fool yourself this dinner is part of the romance of the trip. You're in a Red Lobster, disconnected from the world, what you wanted, that purity, that alone-ness, but it isn't anything. You look at the postcard of your book. You should put it away except the waitress hasn't said anything about your book cover yet and that will move things along. You slide the postcard closer to her side of the table, the side she'll walk by to check, hopefully, how you're enjoying your captain-sized meal. You finish your beer and almost start laughing at what a fake you are.

You have not written a good sentence since the book was accepted. You tried to start another book but couldn't sustain the idea. You tried to write some stories, but they all came out wrong. You came back from a bar one night, read over some pages you'd written, and threw your laptop against the wall. You figured you'd get a new one when you came back from your book tour. You figured after being on the road for three weeks, your head would feel clear and you'd have some stories to write. You didn't think your big adventure would be eating at a Red Lobster and endowing a skinny waitress as the potential savior of your trip. You catch yourself shaking your head. You catch the kids at the other table watching you shaking your head. You open your mouth full of chewed shrimp and they look away scared.

Your waitress returns. She asks how you're enjoying your meal. You ask if she likes brutal honesty or if she's just asking out of politeness. She says it's part of her job, that the manager watches to

make sure the servers ask their customers how they like their food.
You ask what else the manager watches, if the manager's some sort
of seaworthy Big Brother to see if she gets the reference. She looks at
you confused. Her mouth parts, just a little, and she looks away. You
wonder what her face looks like when she's coming, if she looks confused or sure, if she looks flushed or pale, if she feels true joy. The last
woman you slept with in NYC asked to see your face when you came.
After, she said you must be a great poker player.

You tell your waitress you've had managers like that, managers
that watch too closely. You tell your waitress she should get her degree
so she can walk when she has to. She says she'll try, as soon as she
saves up some money, as soon as she gets her life in order. You wonder
what kind of disorder she's in. You wonder if her apartment is a mess.
If her bed is made. If she wipes the come from between her legs or if
she lets it stay there and dry. It's time to move this along. You tell the
waitress you're a teacher. You wait a beat. She asks what grade, and
you say, College. She says you look young to be a college teacher. You
tell her your students think the same thing. You don't tell her you fuck
your students in your office. You do tell her you're on a book tour. You
wait a beat. She asks what kind of book, and you say, A novel. You ask
if she's a reader and point to the postcard. She says she doesn't read
enough. She looks at the postcard. She says, Cool. Cool. You've spent
ten years of your life living like shit and finally get a book published
and the editorial comment you get most often is Cool. You don't fault
the waitress for this. You fault yourself for thinking there could be any
other reaction. You tell the waitress you are cool, and she smiles. You
tell her to check out your book.

It's time to close the deal. You ask her name. She says, Sharon.
You ask Sharon if she'd like to join you for a drink after she finishes
her shift. You look in her eyes and she looks away and smiles. You're

thinking she's easy. You're thinking a waitress in a Red Lobster in the suburbs of Chicago has to realize she'll never again get the chance to sleep with a writer, a real writer, with a book and postcards and the requisite NYC cool. She says she can't. She says her boyfriend is picking her up when she's done with her shift and they're going to the movies.

The movies. You love the high when the theater goes dark, the music comes up, the adrenaline of everything's possible when it's all just starting. But you don't love most movies, most of them shit, all plot, no character, easy entertainment at least a little responsible for you living like shit. Money that could go to buy books goes to the price of admission, popcorn, and a Coke. You don't love writer movies where pages just happen, the contract gets signed, the fame begins. Too many movies, glossy and easy, and your waitress is going to leave you for one.

You look at your waitress. You finish your beer. You ask if she loves her boyfriend. You hold her eyes and she holds yours. She doesn't look shy anymore. She says love isn't something she thinks about. You say love is worth thinking about. It comes out like a line. She asks if you're happy. You repeat the word. Happy. You repeat it again the way you feel it. She says, Exactly. You see she's not just a waitress working in a Red Lobster. She's not just a kid with small-time college ambitions, who might take some creative writing classes, compose some vapid poetry or a sentimental story. She's not just a young piece of ass to get your road count to five. You ask her again to make sure. You ask if she loves her boyfriend. She says her boyfriend doesn't hit her, doesn't criticize her, picks her up every night at the end of her shift since her car broke down, takes her to the movies, treats her right, and right now that's all she thinks about. She says if your book is about love she's really not interested. She says she's tired of fiction when it comes to love.

Your book tour's failing. Your on-the-road adventure is just a long, long drive.

You look past her at the driftwood sign.

Romance of the Seas.

You tell her to look at the sign.

You want to tell her maybe she's too young to feel how she feels. You want to tell her maybe settling should come later in life. You want to tell her maybe love isn't always fiction, maybe there was a ship with that name. You don't say any of this. You just tell her to look at the sign.

She looks at the sign.

She says the one word out loud. Romance.

She smiles a different smile. A sarcastic smile. A jaded smile. A smile for herself. Not a smile for you.

My Painting of Me

"I didn't wrap it well," she says.

She's right. She hasn't. The edges are off, the tape a little sloppy, the paper, paper-bag brown. It's three days past Christmas.

I take off the paper, slowly. Underneath it's bubble wrap. I don't pop any bubbles. I remove the wrap and there's me. She's painted my face from a headshot. She hasn't seen me for eleven years. We slept together once. I met her at a party of a college friend. It was a few months after we graduated. She's still friends with him. I don't see him anymore. She tracked me down. We've written emails back and forth for six months.

It looks like me. She's done a good job with the lines of my face, my hair. She's turned the black-and-white photograph to color, good colors, moody colors the way my black-and-white would have been had it been color. She's made my eyes sad. Not cartoon-sad. I put the bubble wrap around the painting.

We go out for drinks. We catch up on eleven years. I walk her back to her hotel. I thank her for the painting, the best gift, I say, the most thoughtful. She wants to kiss. I don't. I don't tell her to look at my buzzed eyes.

When I'm buzzed I go out. Go out more.

I rub my thumb across my lips.

I go to a bar near her hotel.

She's drinking alone. Another she. It looks like vodka tonic. There's a lime wedge. I run, do push-ups in the park, do pull-ups on the scaffolding bars all over the city.

She takes me home. She lives around the block. Her apartment's small but still like home, still warm-looking. My place has a bed, a couch, a desk, nothing on the walls.

Before the sun comes up I'm up. She's asleep. I go to her bathroom. Rub toothpaste on my finger, a brand I've never tried. Dress.

I take the bubble wrap from around my painting of me. I take down one of her paintings and hang my painting of me.

Outside there's a discarded Christmas tree on the sidewalk. There's still tinsel stuck in its needles. I take a strand and curl it over my top lip. I'm still drunk. I have a tinsel moustache, thin, like his in Goya's, but he's looking up.

the reefing line

It wasn't just the time difference. I woke with the light every morning, the sun rising closer to seven than six, unobstructed unless an Ionian island was in the way that day. I was yachting with my friend Cleo. She worked harder than I did, sixty-hour weeks at the Federal Reserve, which gave her the right to sleep in. She'd sailed before. She could miss the sunrise.

Some mornings I felt too tired to get up. The light would wake me and I'd open my eyes and see through my small cabin window that night was done. I could have fallen back to sleep in a moment, but these were the Greek Islands. When I traveled, I lived, and that meant not doing all the non-living things I did in New York. Sleeping too much. Drinking too much. Hunting for sex. Starving myself so I was lean and mean, so I could drink cheaper and last longer. So I forced myself to stand, to leave the cabin, to climb on deck, to watch the sun touch the horizon, a sliver of burning that seemed to lose its intensity as it rose. In New York, I never saw the sun rise. My sublet faced west, not east, and the horizon was all buildings. Sunsets weren't really sunsets. When the sun went down over the rows of top floors, there was at least an hour of daylight left.

Cleo and I fooled around for a month but we both realized, both quickly, it wasn't right. No one was right, slowly or quickly, for me. I'd been a successful bachelor for years. Then I got bored of being a successful bachelor and got married. Then I missed my bachelor days too much. Six months after our justice-of-the-peace wedding, I left my wife and went back to where I'd been. I met Cleo when my marriage, or what I remembered of my marriage, felt more movie than real.

Cleo and I got along well, very well. We broke the let's-just-be-friends cliché and became real friends, traveling friends. We'd lounged in Cancun. We'd gambled in Vegas. We'd skied in Vail. Now we were sailing in Greece. Calm seas. Light winds. Cleo had given me an early birthday present of sailing lessons at the Hudson River pier, a few blocks from her downtown office. The winds had been calm on the Hudson too, and after my three-day course I'd said to her, How hard can it be? She said sailing could be hard, that strong winds hurt people, that people fell off boats, but I didn't believe her. Sometimes Cleo exaggerated her life. Three days on the Hudson. Eight days on the Ionian. Eleven sailing days total, all of them easy.

Pink streaks underlined the sun. We'd been keeping a list of sailing expressions since the flotilla trip started. *Ship-shape. Yeoman's work. All hands on deck. Down the hatch. A different tack.* The two I kept repeating, over and over, were *Shiver me timbers*, which I delivered in my best Popeye, and *Chips Ahoy*, which I said at the beginning of each day's sail. Cleo would shake her head and tell me to check the anchor. The pink-streaked sky reminded me of the obvious. *Red sky at night, sailors delight. Red sky at morning, sailors take warning.* How hard could it be? Yachts were built not to tip over. Land was in sight at all times. We were both good swimmers. And the flotilla crew were competent, ship-shape Brits with even tempers even when hungover. They could bail us out of any sailing situation.

We'd had another couple on board for drinks the night before. Garrick and Jocelyn. Two true Brits with truly British names, celebrating their third wedding anniversary. It was the first flotilla for both of them, and they'd asked Cleo questions about her other sailing trips. Then the conversation turned to marriage. Cleo told them I was jaded.

I told them I was smart. I caught Jocelyn looking at me and I looked back until she moved her eyes.

Empty plastic cups littered the boat, starboard side. Starboard. Port. Fore. Aft. Main sheet. Genoa sheet. Main halyard. Genoa halyard. I hated the words. I hated the knots. I hated the details. I just wanted to get the sails up when we sailed, fast as I could, and sail. And when the day was done, I wanted to get the sails down fast, get to the dock fast, moor fast. Then we could shower, eat, and drink. After the first day, I'd checked sailing off the list of things I had to do in life. I could now tell the story of the time I'd yachted around the Greek islands.

Chips ahoy. Shiver me timbers.

I wasn't sure if I'd spoken out loud.

The sun rose a latitudinal degree above the horizon and the morning march to the taverna bathrooms began.

I did one hundred push-ups, one hundred sit-ups, punching my stomach during the last ten. My book, which I'd left on board, had a water ring on the cover. Someone had used it as a coaster the night before. I opened to where I'd stuck the boarding pass for British Airways flight 638 to mark the page. I'd read Homer once, years ago, in college. *The Odyssey*. We'd been sailing in Greece for eight days. I was only on page fourteen. I started skimming the lines.

Cleo came up in shorts and a new top for the day. It was light green and showed off her brown skin. She was dark from days of sun, darker than I was and I was dark. My blond hair had turned blonder. When I was a kid, during summer, days and days in the pool, my hair was so blond the chlorine tinted my towhead green.

"Sleep well?"

"I slept great. I was exhausted," she said.

An older couple from the flotilla walked by and we said our

good mornings. I liked hearing their accent. It made me feel far from home. I guessed Cleo was happy to hear British too. Cleo's parents had recently moved to New York from Cairo and were driving her crazy with their bickering. And my nights of going out, drinking hard, waking sick, dressing fast and leaving quickly had been beating me down. We both needed breaks from the States.

"I'm getting some coffee." Cleo stretched her arms to the sky, which was wide and blue. There'd hardly been a cloud all trip. "Do you want to come along, or do you want some more alone time?"

"Let's go."

"I heard you doing sit-ups on deck."

I put down *The Odyssey* and punched my stomach for her.

"Not impressed," she said.

"I'm still in fighting shape."

"Who are you fighting?"

"We're sailing to Ithaca today. It's me against Odysseus."

"My money's on Odysseus," she said.

"You've got no faith."

"I've got faith. You're the one without faith. I still think Odysseus would kick your ass."

"Think of it," I said. "We're actually sailing to Ithaca today. *Pluto* is sailing to Ithaca."

"*Pluto* may not make it to Ithaca."

Pluto was the name of our boat. The water pump leaked. The tiller handle was cracked. The radio didn't work. Our flotilla leader, Amelia, had tried getting the Sunsail people to replace *Pluto* with a more seaworthy boat, but it was summer, all the flotillas were at sea, and the Sunsail executives weren't budging. They kept telling Amelia they'd see what they could do, but so far they'd done nothing. Cleo had already written out a complaint form and we'd been scheming how to make Sunsail pay when the trip was done. I suggested blowing up the boat with the on-board flares.

We jumped off *Pluto*, deck to dock. All the yachts were lined up, tied in, anchored down, looking orderly, as if they'd effortlessly fit into place. I now knew better, knew the hassle of parking a boat, dropping an anchor, tying a seaworthy knot. August in Greece meant too many tourists, too many boats. We walked to the farthest tavern and took a table outside overlooking the sea. Cleo ordered coffee.

"Tell me about Odysseus," Cleo said.

"What do you want to know? He fought for ten years. Then it took him ten years to sail home. His wife waited for him the whole time."

"Good for her."

"Good for him. He was fucking a goddess."

Cleo looked out at the water.

"A ten-year flotilla," she said.

"Ten years, and he was only coming from Troy. He kept running into obstacles, or sailing into them. One-eyed giants. Deadly women singing beautiful songs. Whirlpools and multi-headed monsters."

"Ten years at sea doesn't sound bad, even with all the hassles."

"You know what Odysseus used to say to himself every morning before he set sail?"

"What?"

"*How hard can it be?*"

"You're an idiot."

"Why does that bother you so much?"

"Because you don't realize how dangerous it can get out there."

I put out my hand, kept my hand steady.

"That means nothing," Cleo said. "By the way, fear makes us human."

"Speaking of humans and fear, I think you scared away our Brit friends last night talking about all your boating mishaps."

"You're the one who scared them."

"Not me."

"You were drunk. You said some mean things. You probably don't remember."

"What did I say?"

"You kept going off on marriage. You kept telling them how lust fades, how it's inevitable, how people stay together because they're weak. You said you'd checked off marriage on your list and you'd never do it again. You didn't stop. You told Jocelyn she didn't seem like the marrying type. It's their third wedding anniversary. They didn't need to hear your cynical shit."

"They're old enough to hear it and know it. They're not kids. If you were so upset, you should have countered my cynical shit with your romantic shit."

"I'd rather be romantic than cynical."

The coffee came. Cleo added a cube of sugar, stirred.

"Very symbolic."

"Actually, the coffee's bitter like your outlook on life."

"You know she likes me," I said.

"No. She doesn't like you."

"She does."

"You think everybody likes you."

"It's amazing, isn't it? Lights. Camera. Action. Jocelyn was checking me out the whole night. I remember that much."

Cleo stopped talking.

I watched the waiters move between tables.

She finished her coffee.

"The sky was red this morning," I said. "You missed it."

"I've seen red skies," Cleo said. "Let's go back to the boat and get our map. The group meeting's in fifteen minutes."

"Pleasant Amelia with her pleasant good mornings."

"It's pleasant to be pleasant," Cleo said. "Maybe you can be the pleasant captain this morning and chart our course for the day."

Ithaca was in sight.

Steeper than the other islands, more rocky, more brutal, it looked like the place I'd read about. Homer had done his homework. I was at the helm. Cleo was sitting near me, reading her novel, hat and sunglasses shading her face from the sun. The radio, tuned to a Greek station, was playing an upbeat song with lots of strings. Then the wind hit. A quick gust filled the main sail, a second gust filled the Genoa sail, white faces stretched taut, too taut, too full, and I saw, heard, felt the power. Cleo had already put down her book. She was working one of the ropes, the one with the red stripe.

"Hold it hard," she said.

I assumed she meant the tiller. It was bucking, pulling. Cleo pulled the rope tight.

"What rope is that?" I said.

"It's called a sheet."

"It's still a rope."

"Both hands on the tiller."

The wind hit again, more than a gust, a steady, too-heavy press. I looked at the gauge on top of the mast. I was holding the tiller and looking up, my legs off-balance, the wind pressing my eyes.

"Hold it steady," Cleo was yelling.

I was looking at the gauge, looking at the sky, trying to judge the wind. The boat was turning. The press got louder, a wall of low whistle, wind against sail. Something came fast. I heard more than felt.

I wasn't holding the tiller anymore. My shoulder hurt. My sunglasses were off. I was sitting against the side of the boat. The boat pulled the other way. The boom shot past my head the other way. She was on the tiller turning the boat. I held onto the rail.

The boat steadied. The sails filled. I stood. I wiped my hand across the bridge of my nose. I was bleeding.

"You can't move the back of the boat into the wind," she was yelling.

Blood filled the lines in my hand. I wanted to punch something back. I was dizzy. It felt like a fight.

"That's how hard it can be," she was yelling.

The rest of the afternoon was a disaster. Cleo tried to teach me how to sail in strong winds, but I didn't care. Three days of sailing lessons and eight days of calm seas hadn't prepared me for this. She was testing me. It felt like she was testing me and I hated tests. Main sheet. Main halyard. Genoa furl. Beam reach. Broad reach. Reefing line. Kicker. I didn't fucking care. I said it out loud sometimes, said it out loud many times. To friends. To family. To women when I walked out of their lives. I don't care. I don't fucking care.

The scenery was spectacular, the island of Kefalonia behind us, the island of Ithaca rising in front, the cleanest sea, between aqua and green, all around. History. Beauty. Miles away from too-busy Manhattan. But I didn't fucking care.

"How hard can it be?" she said. "You almost had your head taken off."

"It's just wind. I wasn't ready. It's not even fun."

"It's not fun for me either. I feel like I'm sailing this thing alone."

"I'll put the engine on. I'll drive this piece of shit to wherever the fuck we're going."

"Where are we going?"

"You wrote it down."

"That's the point. Not you. I wrote it down."

Cleo stayed looking at me, her mouth tight, then looked away. She furled, coiled, whatever the fuck you called it, she did that to the front sail, the fucking Genoa sail, on her own. She climbed across the boat, held the boom, got the main sail down.

"Go ahead," she said.

"Go ahead what?"

"That's what you wanted. Start the engine."

I could do that. I climbed down to the cabin. My shoulder ached, the top of my arm. I switched on the power. I climbed back up, flicked the switch, and the engine started. Our boat, masts bare, no better than a motorboat now, moved pitifully forward to Ithaca. I looked at all the other yachts, sails taut and proud, gliding over the sea. From a distance it looked fun. From a distance it looked easy.

I steered the boat. We didn't speak. Cleo was probably calculating how quickly she could leave Greece, leave me, fly back to New York.

"You're a bully," she said. "Whenever you don't like something, or whenever you're outside your comfort zone, instead of accepting that maybe things can get a little uncomfortable, or that maybe you need to try a little harder, you take it out on the people around you."

We were back on shore. Ithaca's shore. The boat was docked and we were sitting on deck. We hadn't spoken while we showered and changed, but I'd mixed us each a strong gin and tonic, then another, and Cleo's hard face softened, though not much. It had been a shit day.

"You are," she said. "You're a bully."

"You didn't tell me it was going to be like this."

"There you go."

"You didn't."

"*How hard can it be? How hard can it be?* Now you know."

I was too cocky sometimes, but it was more than that. I was stronger than she was. Faster. More coordinated. If she could do it, I could do it too. Whatever adventures Cleo had had, and she'd had many, they couldn't be that amazing, that difficult. Maybe I was jealous of all the traveling she'd done before we'd met, all the far-off places she'd seen, all the challenges she'd taken. India. China. The Galapagos Islands. A safari through the Serengeti. A jeep trip across the Sinai. Hiking in Laos and Cambodia. Climbing Mount Kilimanjaro. Maybe it was my way to dismiss her life before me, a part of her life, a part she genuinely seemed to love. I could relegate her travels to a checklist. I could relegate everyone's lives, everyone's loves, to justify my day-to-day not-living, which I'd done for too long. I pretended my not-living was fine, was worthy, was an adventure itself. When travelers bragged too much and asked me where I'd been, I'd tell them I'd visited more pussy than they'd ever visit, that I'd played around the world with hundreds of women from everywhere, that my adventure was bedding one woman after another woman after another. I didn't need to prove myself with a checklist of where I'd been and what I'd done. My checklist was cunt. I could do anyone, so I could do anything. If Cleo could sail, I could sail. But when the first true wind hit, I got sucker punched. But it wasn't a sucker punch. It was a swinging boom, fair and square, square into me.

"I'm going to have another. Do you want another?"

"Don't get too drunk," she said.

"I'm not drunk."

"Then you'll be mean all over again."

"I'm done being mean."

"You'll start bullying."

I held up my empty glass and started backing down the hatch. Each rung hurt my shoulder.

"One more," she said. "Make me one more. We should eat."

"What are you craving?"

"You choose. You're the one with the sailing injury."

"*Shiver me timbers*."

"Great," she said. "You were a real Popeye today."

"I'll tell you what I'm really craving."

"Spinach."

"Nope."

"Tell me."

"Greek food."

Cleo smiled, she had a great smile, and like that we were best friends again. She tossed me her empty cup, plastic, no breakables on board.

I climbed down the rest of the way. The bottle of Tanqueray was already on the counter, the bag of ice open, the lime cut. I poured two drinks, stiff, squeezed extra lime in her glass the way she liked, used one hand to hold the glasses, one hand to hold the ladder to climb on deck. I was buzzed. I felt I could beat the world.

We drank. We laughed at our day. I had to be careful not to push the joking too hard. Cleo got mad quickly, too quickly for me. When I was married my wife got mad too quickly, I remembered that, so I left. I didn't feel like leaving Greece, not yet. So I didn't push things, didn't force Cleo's smile away. When we drank, and when her smile disappeared, she'd list my transgressions. The time I criticized her friend so harshly about her fiancé, her friend broke down crying. I'd been drunk. The time I stomped a guy's bare toes because I didn't like him wearing flip flops in a bar. I'd been drunk. The time I stranded her between two desolate avenues at 4 a.m., pissed at something. I'd been drunk. So I drank my gin and tonic and watched what I said. I didn't want to hear the list. Not from her. She wasn't my wife. I'd had a wife and I'd run.

"What are we eating?" Cleo said.

"I want octopus. We should order two orders. And that spinach pie. We don't even need a main dish. Let's just order hundreds of appetizers."

"Hundreds."

"And I want a Mythos. Two Mythos. Let's sail drunk tomorrow."

"No," she said, and I checked myself, left it alone.

We jumped deck to dock and walked hand in hand to the row of restaurants. People thought we were boyfriend and girlfriend.

The dishes were gone. The glasses remained. The day, the wind, the arguments, the disgust, the making-up that wasn't quite made up, it all needed alcohol. We were drunk. Mythos beers turned to shots of ouzo that went down licorice-sweet, whiskey warm. I almost forgot the swinging boom. She almost forgot my bullying. We'd eaten Greek salad with tomatoes so red, so perfectly ripe, they really were fruits, not vegetables. We'd eaten octopus and skewers of lamb and a whole grilled red snapper. We'd laughed about past days on past trips, good days. The moon was low in the sky and thin, many nights into waning.

Garrick and Jocelyn walked by.

He was holding her around. She was laughing. They were both a little red-faced.

"You should make nice after your diatribe the other night," Cleo said. "It's their third anniversary. I think it's sweet. I think they look sweet together."

"I think you're drunk."

"I'm on vacation."

"Whatever."

"Don't be a bully," she said, and she stood and waved them over.

"This wasn't what we decided," I said. "We were supposed to hang out alone tonight."

"There are lots of things we didn't decide. Look at your nose."

Cleo was social even when sober, but this had nothing to do with being social. She wanted me to show her something. I wasn't in the mood to apologize for what I'd said, whatever I'd said, about marriage the night before. Just like I wasn't in the mood to beg forgiveness for my day's transgressions. I touched the bridge of my nose. The scab felt wet. Blood smudged my finger.

"Good to see you," Cleo said, talking to them, not me.

Garrick took two chairs from an empty table and placed them between Cleo and me. He made a big production out of seating Jocelyn first. When he sat, his knee was too close to my knee.

"What happened to you?" he said, leaning forward to inspect my face.

"You should have seen the other guy."

"You had a fist fight? It was the Italians, wasn't it? They're animals."

"He was hit by the boom," Cleo said.

I looked at Cleo. I looked at Garrick.

"Now you know. I got hit by the boom."

"That must have hurt," Garrick said.

"How hard can it be?" Cleo said.

I called the waiter over. I ordered eight shots of ouzo. If Cleo wanted a party, we'd have a party.

"How did you guys do out there?" Cleo said.

"It was a bit rough today, wasn't it?" Garrick was squinting, playing the sun-scorched sailor. "We weathered the gusts quite well after a few mishaps. Before we left home, our friends reckoned if we could get through a yachting holiday together our marriage would last forever."

"So far, so good," I said. "*Red sky at morning, sailors take warning.*"

Garrick took Jocelyn's hand. I could see him squeezing it. Like *I love you.* Like *Sailing is nothing compared to the strength of our commitment.* Like *Let's just hear what this asshole has to say, drink a shot or two, then head back to our yacht.*

"So far, so good," I said again.

I felt Cleo watching me. The waiter came with our shots.

"What should we toast?" I said.

"Health and happiness," Garrick said.

"Let's try for something more original. We're in Greece. We're in Ithaca."

"What's wrong with health and happiness?" Cleo said.

"It's been done."

"What do you propose?"

"I'll tell you what I propose. I propose we drink to heavy winds tomorrow. I want to get some revenge on the fucker that did this to me."

"You did it to yourself," Cleo said.

"That's it then. I propose a toast to myself. Here's to me."

I raised my glass and moved it forward and by instinct they moved their glasses forward, glasses against glasses, and the toast was official. The ouzo went down warm. I watched their faces. Garrick took it. Jocelyn took it with a quick purse of her lips. I didn't look at Cleo. She could sail like a sailor and drink like a sailor. I'd gone through bottles with her. We had a history in bars.

"And to me again," I said and lifted the second shot. Only Garrick joined me. Cleo and Jocelyn left the two remaining glasses on the table.

"No?" I said.

I was looking at Cleo.

"I've had enough," she said.

"More for us."

I touched glasses with Garrick, drank.

"So what got you through the day?" I said. "What got you through the wind? The two of you haven't sailed much more than I have."

"We used the reefing line," Garrick said. "We cut the sail in half."

"You cut it in half?"

"You know. We reduced the sail. With the reefing line."

"Which line is that?"

"It's one of the two middle lines in our boat. The blue-striped line. I don't know which line it is in yours."

"No worries," Cleo said like she was suddenly British. "He doesn't know which line it is either."

Garrick smiled, red-faced. "It can take some time. It took Jocelyn a while too. We've been quizzing each other."

"How does that work out for you?" I said. "Me, I hate getting quizzed. I hate getting tested."

"We make a game of it."

"A game. I like games better than quizzes. Let's hear the game?"

"It's private," Jocelyn said. It was the first time she'd spoken.

"Why's that? Is it some sort of sex quiz?"

Garrick laughed too loud, an easy tell. The ouzo had hit him. His hand was on Jocelyn's thigh. She hadn't looked at me since she'd sat down, but now she was looking. I looked at her. Put the image right in her eyes. It was my hand on her thigh. My hand moving up her thigh. My hand touching her cunt.

"It is a sex quiz," I said. "Why don't you give me one of your quiz questions? I know sex. That's my best subject. In fact, why don't we play for some stakes? With a little sex, I might end up remembering all this bullshit sailing terminology."

"Enough," Cleo said.

This wasn't the boardroom. She wasn't running a meeting. I'd never listen to her orders.

Jocelyn took Garrick's ouzo glass from his hand, inspected it, drank the few drops left, put the glass on the table.

"It's not bullshit terminology," Jocelyn said. "Not if you want to use the wind."

"What does that mean?"

"My husband saw you."

"Your husband saw me?"

"My husband saw you through the glasses. You didn't have your sails up."

I felt my face fill with blood. I didn't care, but I did. It had been a perfect day for sailing, but we hadn't sailed. I breathed into it. I wasn't looking at Jocelyn's eyes. I was looking at the bridge of her nose. My hand was a fist.

"There's a reason we weren't sailing."

"Really?" Jocelyn said. "I'm curious. What was the reason?"

"We were playing our own game."

"What game was that?"

She was pushing. I always pushed. That's what bullies did. They pushed.

"It wasn't a sex game," I said. "Cleo and I don't play those."

"No, we don't," Cleo said.

"What was it?" Jocelyn said.

"We were reenacting the myth."

"The myth?"

"From *The Odyssey*. From when Odysseus returns to Ithaca. I remembered the story and we played it out. His son threw himself into the sea when he saw there were no sails on his father's ship. If the sails were up, it meant Odysseus was alive. If the sails were down, it meant Odysseus was dead. That was their code for when Odysseus returned home. Sails, alive. No sails, dead. He'd been at sea for ten years and Odysseus forgot to put up his sails. It was a fatal mistake. His son was so grief-stricken, he dove into the Ionian Sea and drowned."

Jocelyn laughed. I'd never heard her laugh before.

"You wanted to reenact a mistake? You wanted to pretend you forgot?"

"Forgetting is more interesting than remembering," I said. "If you keep forgetting, everything seems new."

"To forgetting," Garrick said.

I didn't look at him. I was looking at Jocelyn. She was smiling.

"That's not the story," she said. "You forgot the story. It was Theseus, not Odysseus. It was black sails, not no sails. It was the Aegean sea, not the Ionian. It was his father, not his son. I always loved mythology as a girl, and I remember all the stories."

"Excellent," Cleo said.

"You lost the game," Garrick said.

Now I was looking at the bridge of Garrick's nose.

"I don't care."

"I think you do," Cleo said.

"Don't be a bully."

"How hard can it be?"

"Double or nothing," I said.

"I didn't know we'd agreed to play for stakes," Jocelyn said.

I raised my hand to the waiter, four fingers in the air.

"Don't worry. It's not a drinking game."

"I'm not worried," Garrick said.

"You're drunk, aren't you?"

"I'm a bit pissed," he said.

He'd lined up the empty glasses on the table.

"We're all a bit pissed," Cleo said, trying to make nice.

"Double or nothing." My voice was too loud.

I watched the waiter carry the tray. I watched him set down the glasses. I lifted one without a toast, downed it.

"Here's the next question," I said. "We'll see how much my-thology you remember. How many women did Odysseus fuck?"

Jocelyn raised her hand like she was in class. She was pushing it. Bullies all around.

"That's easy," Jocelyn said. "More than you."

"Well played," Garrick said loud, laughed.

Jocelyn smiled for her husband.

I waited for her eyes to come back to my eyes.

"Want to bet?" I said.

"Bet what?" Jocelyn said. "What could you possibly give me?"

Garrick was laughing again, loud, red-faced, his hand on her thigh.

I stood. I put my hands on the table. I wanted to make a point.

I was standing, leaning forward. I wanted to make a point but forgot what point I wanted to make.

"Your cut is bleeding," Cleo said.

I touched my face, looked at the blood, didn't care.

"You're drunk," Cleo said.

I saw it, drunk saw it. Flying back to New York. Saying Fuck it for real. Cutting everyone off. Never talking to anyone I knew again, never. That's how I'd done it with my wife. I cut her off as soon as I moved out. I forgot all about her and went back to what I'd done before.

I was already standing.

I moved my hands from the table.

I started walking.

Walking back to the yacht. Walking back to *Pluto*. No one following me.

The Sunsail yachts were docked all in a row.

The sky was dark, not red.

"*Chips ahoy*," I said. I was talking loud, talking out loud. "*Chips ahoy*."

I struggled with the ropes, thick ropes, struggled to loosen the knots. I wasn't good with knots. Hitches. Fucking hitches. The rope was too fucking thick.

I loosened and pulled and pulled and threw the ropes on the boat.

I pushed against the boat and felt it move.

The space got bigger, the space of water under me, and I jumped, deck to dock.

I knew how to start the engine. I knew how to use the tiller. It wasn't much different from steering a car. I went down, started the engine, came up, flicked the switch. I kept my hands steady on the tiller. The boat moved forward. I pushed the throttle. The boat moved faster. I was out of the harbor.

I pushed the throttle harder. I looked back and saw the line of Sunsail yachts, the row of restaurants lit up, the mountains behind, steep mountains, Ithaca's mountains. It took him ten years to get home. Maybe he forgot so much it seemed new again. Maybe he remembered so much he did everything he could not to come back too quickly.

I drove the boat out to sea, far enough where the lights were small, where I could see other lights of other towns.

It wasn't windy. I wanted it to be windy, but it wasn't. I shut the engine. It took a while, but I got the sails up. I didn't know the names of the ropes. I didn't know the names. But I got them up. Then I sat down at the back of the boat with my hand on the tiller.

After a while I took my hand off the tiller. There was no wind and the boat didn't move. It just stayed there in the middle of the sea. There was nobody around. Nobody. What Polyphemus screamed after Odysseus stabbed out his eye. Who did this? the other giants asked Polyphemus when they saw their blinded leader. Nobody, Polyphemus screamed in agony. That was the name Odysseus had given himself. Nobody. That was the story. I almost had the other story right. I thought I'd had it right. The sailing story.

The boat didn't move.

I sat there, in *Pluto*, in the sea, in the dark.

I could go down and get the flares. I could light one up, watch it rise into the sky, a call for help while late-night drinkers finished their last drinks. I could touch the bridge of my nose, rip at the scab, paint my fingers with blood. Or I could sit, just sit and wait, just sit and watch until the sun rose.

last straws

I don't register the purple discoloration under Patrick's eye until I say hello and he looks up. He's wearing sunglasses, but the shiner spreads under the frame, a murky half-moon that fades into his cheekbone. He smiles his yellow-toothed smile that always seems pitiful, but it's hard to pity him. We shake hands. His grip is weak and sweaty.

"How are you?" he says, upbeat, the lilt making his soft voice sound even more Irish. It's clear Patrick isn't doing too well.

The people coming out of Citarella carry full bags of fresh produce, artisanal cheeses, prepared pastas, homemade breads and desserts. There's something happily domestic about their purchases on a Saturday afternoon and I can picture the various delicacies presented on platters in their living rooms, smiling family and friends standing around, talking, eating, thinking this is the life.

"What are you doing in this neighborhood?" I say.

"Walking about."

"It's a great day for that."

"There you are," Patrick says. "I shouldn't have worn my jacket. It's a bit warm."

"I guess I don't mind the heat. Have you seen Mike?"

Mike is our connection. Patrick knows Mike from when they taught together in the same school before Mike moved from elementary to high school. I know Mike from the Thomas Jefferson Boxing Club. Most afternoons, we were the only White guys hitting the heavy bags and after we sparred the first time we went out for beers. Now we drink together more, work out together less. I've met Patrick a couple of times. At Mike's bachelor party. At Mike's wedding.

"I haven't seen him recently," Patrick says. "Have you?"

"I saw him Thursday. He's looking forward to starting school."

"He was waiting to hear when we last spoke."

"He got in. NYU Law. If we ever get in trouble, we'll know the man to call."

"True," Patrick says.

Patrick shifts his feet. It's 80 degrees out, a weekend short of Memorial Day, but he's wearing corduroys, heavy shoes, a windbreaker over a button shirt and a T-shirt under that. Maybe it's winter in the Bronx.

"What's new with you, then?" Patrick says. "Are you still at the college?"

"Still teaching. My students get worse each semester. There's no such thing as English Composition anymore. It's Run-on Sentences and Grammatical Errors 101."

"The students are not too bright, then?"

"A few are great. Too many aren't even dim."

"I miss teaching some days."

"You should get back into it."

"I get on where I am. I finish by four every afternoon. One of my bosses, he's a bit difficult, but usually I can do my work without bother."

"He doesn't touch you, does he?"

"No. Not him. None of that."

I know from Mike that Patrick now works as a janitor at a junior high. When he'd taught, his fourth graders supposedly liked him, but I could hear the kids calling him Patricia, something fourth-grader smart like that. He'd been yelled at during a PTA meeting for forcing a

disruptive student to sit in the corner, and the administration had termi-
nated his position over the winter break, claiming financial difficulties.
According to Mike, Patrick's year had been a spiraling fall from grace.
He'd gone from schoolteacher to janitor. He'd left a nice apartment in
Riverdale to move in with a horrible woman in the Bronx. She worked
in a laundromat. She was mean and loud. Maybe she was beating the
shit out of Patrick after bad days folding people's underwear and socks.

"Report the guy if he bothers you too much," I say.

"I know."

"What is he, the head janitor or something?"

"He's in charge, yes."

"File a complaint."

"I know," Patrick says.

He looks at his feet and maybe he sees his year-long fall down
there, heavy shoes against the backdrop of pavement, shoes he probably wears while mopping tiled corridors or scraping gum from under
desks. Patrick's bent neck, his slightly curved back, his loose hanging
arms spell defeat.

"I'm showing the Holyfield fight at my apartment tonight.
Some guys are coming over and Mike will be there. Why don't you
come by?"

"Luz cooks dinner on Saturdays," Patrick says.

And she beats the shit out of you on Fridays, I think, pronounc-
ing shit *shite* in my head the way the Irish do.

"Tell her to keep it warm for you," I say.

"I don't know," Patrick says.

"Come on, Patrick. Boys night out. Beer. Booze. An interesting
fight. You'll have fun."

"Sure I would."

"I'll tell you what. I'll speak to what's her name. Luz. I'll speak to Luz. I'll tell her you need a boys night out with the boys. You look like you could use a night."

"I could at that," he says, and smiles weakly.

"Mike said you gave up the drink," he says.

"For a while. I went to AA a few times. It wasn't for me."

"Now you've started again?"

"I've cut down," I say.

I had stopped. Again. I was getting into trouble again, going too far. Then, the way my cycle went, I stopped the stopping. I started sweet. White Russians. Two shots Stoli. One shot Kahlua. Milk. I'd have two or three. A vodka shot before I went out. I'd missed the happy that came with that first sip, the more-happy that came with more. I missed the bars, moving from one to the next, meeting many, choosing one, sweating out the alcohol with a new body in bed, not knowing who it was, a feeling I wanted, then waking, peeing out the rest of my drunk, rubbing toothpaste, sometimes a flavor I'd never tasted, against my teeth and tongue, picking my clothes from the floor, getting dressed, leaving, and sometimes I didn't know what street I was on, another feeling I wanted, a morning-after scene and the camera all on me and everything I'd done right there in my eyes, and I'd look for a marker, a building, a park, try to guess where I was before I got to the corner, saw the sign.

"Tonight I'm letting loose. It's Holyfield's last fight. He's old, but he's still got heart and a pair of balls. We need to drink to his last fight. I want to see him beat this young punk and retire with a win."

"It should be a good fight, then?"

"Come over. You'll have a good time."

"I was planning on walking about the city for a while."

"Walk about and come by about nine."

"I'll try, then."

"Try hard. Mike will tell you about the career counselor he met at NYU. It's a funny story. There should be plenty of beer."

"Grand," Patrick says.

We shake hands. Patrick turns and walks slowly off. I go into Citarella, wipe Patrick's sweat from my palm, head to the meat counter for soppressata sausage.

I unpack the groceries and give Mike a call. For some reason his wife answers, but she's good about keeping the small talk small and hands over the phone. I tell Mike I've seen Patrick and he has a black eye. I listen to Mike repeat the news to his wife.

"He was wearing sunglasses," I say. "But the shiner was peeking out in all its glory."

"That bitch is hitting him now. I'm sure of it. I told you about the cats, didn't I?"

"What cats?"

"She's got cats. After Patrick moved into her place, she picked up some Siamese cats even though she knew Patrick was allergic to them. He asked her to find the cats a new home, but that Luz bitch wouldn't get rid of them. One night Patrick started wheezing and an ambulance had to take him to the hospital. He almost died. Right afterward, when Patrick was still pissed off, I spoke to him, and he said the cats were the last straw, but she still has the cats."

"The last straw," I repeat in my best Irish accent, impersonating Patrick's weak voice. "I sneezed me last sneeze and those bastard Siamese are the last straw."

"She encourages him to keep his janitor job," Mike says. "She makes him help her out at the laundromat after he's put in a full day's work. She took all his savings and gave the money to her own mother so her mother could move to Orlando. She kicks him out of the house some nights and leaves him to wander around the Bronx until morning. Now she's beating the shit out of him. I hope this will be the last straw."

"I don't know. He sounded like he was going back for more."

"I've got to talk to him. She'll end up killing the poor bastard."

Outside a siren starts at the fire house and gets louder. My Bedford Street studio is on the direct route between the station and Eighth Avenue. I live on the third floor of a five-flight walk-up. I've never really moved in, don't have pictures on the walls or photographs showing family or friends. I spend most nights somewhere else. My place is a place, anonymous, all I need, somewhere to catch up on sleep, shower, change my clothes, start my nights. When I fold up the futon, it's just a couch, a small table, two chairs, and a big screen TV, which we'll crowd around tonight when the bell rings. Sometimes the siren sounds like more than a warning. Sometimes, when it wakes me, I can't get back to sleep. I wait for the truck to pass, the sound to fade.

"You still there?"

"I'm here," Mike says.

"I invited Patrick to come over."

"Is he coming?"

"He said he'd try."

"That means nothing. Where did you see him?"

"Downtown. Outside Citarella."

"Did you pick up those cheese sticks I like?"

"I got them."

"He probably went over to Dempsey's. They serve Murphy's Stout. It reminds him of home. I'll try to find him and talk some sense into him. I've got to convince him to get out of the Bronx."

"Savior of the day," I say.

"He needs to be saved."

"And you're just the man to save him."

"Definitely more man than you."

"That's it. That's the last straw."

We say goodbye. The futon isn't folded up yet. It's four hours to fight time. I'm still hung over and tired from another one night stand. I left her place at five in the morning, drank Yoo-Hoo on the subway to settle my stomach, slept on and off until noon. I set the alarm for seven and lie down. I wonder what Holyfield is doing. If he's resting. If he's looking in the mirror to see how strong his muscles look. If he's thinking about his opponent. If he's feeling old. Holyfield says it's his last fight and when it's over he'll put his millions in the bank. Millions. Whenever we're sitting around the TV, watching a pay-per-view fight, one of the guys invariably says he'd step in the ring and have the shit beat out of him for just one million. A broken nose or a shattered cheekbone is worth it. I used to respond to their stupid hypotheticals. If they were afraid to fight on the street for free, how would they fight a professional in front of a crowd? That's the kind of loss too hard to face. You can't make up a story to smooth over the defeat when everyone was there, when everyone saw you get your ass kicked. And no one would pay money to see such a one-sided fight. The odds are 3 to 1 against Holyfield but Holyfield is Holyfield, he has a history of heart behind him, he's fought as a champion many times, and if this really is his last fight, he deserves whatever he can make.

"Holy, Holy,, Holyfield," I say out loud.

I fantasize about him finishing strong, a clean knock-out punch flush on the younger man's jaw. I see him raising his hands for the final time. And I feel myself going out.

Steve shows up first. It's 8:45 and he carries a six-pack of beer and a bag full of snacks. Barbecue potato chips. Doritos. Dipsy Doodles. It's the kind of shit I never eat, which is why I'm in better shape than all of them, why my students still look at me. I put the beer in the fridge, pop one for myself, one for Steve. Jason shows at 9:00 with two six-packs. The pay-per-view channel comes on. There's the usual pre-fight hype. I keep the sound low and the three of us catch up. The buzzer rings and five minutes later Klemmer walks in out of breath with two six-packs and a forty-ouncer he's already working on.

"These stairs are a killer," Klemmer says.

"Maybe it's time to lose that gut," I say.

"I enjoy my gut," Klemmer says.

The buzzer rings. It has to be Mike.

"Who do you pick?" Klemmer asks the room.

Steve and Jason like the younger fighter. Klemmer says he's also going with the kid. I say I'm going with Holyfield.

"Snacks," Klemmer says and starts loading up on soppressata.

The door opens, Mike walks in and behind him is Patrick. They're each carrying two six-packs. Mike's eyes look buzzed and I guess Patrick's eyes are the same. He's still wearing sunglasses.

"Welcome," I say. "I'm glad you made it, Patrick."

"There was no getting away from Mike."

"I bribed him with Murphy's," Mike says.

"There you are. Murphy's Stout is my weakness," Patrick says and laughs, high-pitched, almost manic, a staccato explosion that peaks then ends abruptly when Patrick covers his mouth.

"How come you never bribe me?" Jason says.

"Because you Wall Street types make too much money to be bribed with beer."

"What about me?" Klemmer says.

"What about you?" Mike says. "You're a drunk. I don't want to be responsible for your swollen liver."

"That's my stomach, not my liver."

I introduce Patrick as an old friend of Mike's. They all say hello and shake Patrick's hand. No one wipes their palm. Maybe Patrick's hands are less sweaty now, now that he's had some drinks, now that he's been away from Luz in the Bronx for more than a few hours. Maybe he's even thought about smacking her back next time she smacks him, but I doubt it. His meek voice. His pitiful smile. I can hear his fourth grade kids. Miss Lally. Patricia Lally. And worse. The introductions are over and Patrick stands in the middle of the room, not sure what to do with himself. I put all the six-packs in the fridge. Mike comes up to me.

"She really beat the shit out of him," Mike whispers.

"You should teach him a few moves. If he throws a well-timed hook to her jaw, maybe she'll think twice before she hits him."

"She's hit him before."

"How can he live with himself?" I say. "He's a man. He's got balls, right? How big is this Luz?"

"She's actually pretty small."

"Anyone want another beer?" I say to the room and Klemmer calls for round two.

I hand Patrick a beer, pull a chair around from the kitchen table, and motion for him to sit. He keeps his windbreaker on. I hand Klemmer a beer. Mike takes a seat on the futon. The first preliminary bout starts, a couple of welterweight contenders fighting for a shot at a title. I keep the sound low. I sit on the floor. We talk about the upcoming fight. We talk about what's new, which isn't much. Klemmer asks Mike if he'll really be able to handle the law school load and Mike says now that he's a married man he better handle it.

"Ball and chain," Klemmer yells, belches, stands, gets another beer.

Steve asks Patrick what he does for a living and Patrick says he does custodial work. He says he used to teach with Mike. He lifts his sunglasses for a moment, rubs his eye.

"It's a burn-out profession," I say.

"I'll drink to that," Mike says. "That's why I'm getting out."

"Lots of luck," Patrick says and drinks.

"What happened to your eye?" Klemmer calls from the fridge.

Sometimes Klemmer is an idiot, but it is a fight night, and it is a black eye, and the more beers we drink, the bigger our muscles get. I've seen these guys almost fight when they're drunk, but they've never come close to fighting sober, and when Mike and I put on the gloves in the gym it's only to spar, punches checked with less than bad intentions.

"I had an accident," Patrick says, and his voice is quiet, quieter than it's been since he arrived.

"You hit someone's fist with your eye?" Klemmer says.

"He got hurt on the job," Mike says. "If you worked more than part time, you'd know something about that."

"I know something about these Dipsy Doodles," Klemmer says and takes a handful.

"What did you used to teach?" Steve asks.

"The little ones," Patrick says. "Fourth grade."

"I had a crush on my fourth grade teacher. Miss Koritowsky. She got married and left town the summer after she was my teacher."

"The one that got away, then," Patrick says.

"There have been plenty of others," Steve says.

"*She lived unknown, and few could know when Lucy ceased to be; but she is in her grave, and, oh, The difference to me!*"

Patrick recites the verse beautifully, almost forcefully. His accent makes it sadder still, adds melancholy to the words *difference* and *me*.

"Where's that from?" Steve says.

"Wordsworth," Patrick says. "The nuns made us memorize him in school."

"What school was that?" Klemmer says.

"Our Lady of Grace. My school back in Ireland."

"I'm a poet and I know it," Klemmer says and walks around with a six-pack, hands each of us a beer. I watch Patrick finish his bottle and reach for a new one. One of the young welterweights on TV takes some punches against the ropes.

Holyfield moves toward the ring, singing a spiritual, his eyes looking toward heaven, his face calm. We're passing around a bottle of tequila. My hangover from this morning has smoothed away. Everyone's talking louder now. When the fight's done, we'll go down to a bar and drink some more and talk about the fight and my eyes will wander. I'll pretend to listen while I check out the women and I'll move to one and concentrate on making the rest of the night last into morning.

"Swing low, sweet chariot," Mike sings.

"Rock my soul in the bosom of Abraham," Steve sings.

"The hills are alive with the sound of music," Klemmer sings.

"That's a show tune," Mike says. "Not a spiritual, you moron."

Patrick laughs, covers his mouth.

I remember a story Mike told. He and Patrick had driven upstate together and while hiking they got lost in the woods. When it started to get dark, Patrick became terrified. He held onto Mike's arm and wouldn't let go. Mike said he couldn't believe it. When they finally got out of the woods and found their bearings, Patrick thanked Mike for not leaving him. He was practically crying and he kept saying Thank you, thank you, thank you.

Holyfield steps into the ring, singing the final verse, the spiritual now background music to the screaming crowd.

"You better pray, old man," Klemmer says.

Klemmer always roots for the up-and-comer. I always root for the underdog. When I started teaching, I gave and gave, trying to help my students progress, master their writing, reach graduation. Many of them had rough lives, city kids grown up too fast, and I wanted them to win. But too many weren't doing their work. And the administration kept piling on our work. Extra committee assignments. Academic advisement. Outcomes assessments that had nothing to do with real outcomes. After a while I didn't try so hard. And I'd started sleeping with my students. One night, right after Mike got engaged, when he and I went drinking after three rounds of sparring, Mike told me I was corrupt. I told him I was a teacher who reaped the benefits of his student bodies. I told him I didn't care how corrupt I was as long as no one found out.

"Who do you want?" I ask Patrick, and I'm genuinely interested, curious if he likes the favorite or the underdog, the young buck or the old warrior.

"I want Holyfield," he says.

"I want him too."

"Would either of you losers like to put money where your mouths are?" Klemmer says.

"You still owe me from last fight," I say.

"I won't owe you for this one," Klemmer says.

"Pass me the tequila," I say and he does and I drink and pass the bottle to Mike and he drinks and passes the bottle to Patrick and Patrick drinks a long swallow and the bottle bumps his sunglasses and for a moment the purple's all there.

"She's a beauty," Klemmer says.

"She?" Patrick says.

"You should put a steak on that eye."

"You don't know her, so don't speak about her."

"Interesting. If that's her M.O., I probably don't want to know her."

"Why don't you shut your fecking mouth," Patrick says. The way he says *fecking* is off-the-boat Irish, not poetic at all.

The room goes quiet.

Patrick adjusts his sunglasses.

"Was that Wordsworth too?" Klemmer says.

"Watch the fight, Klemmer," Mike says. "Let's see if your boy can win."

"You want to bet?"

"Watch the fight," Mike says.

"You afraid you'll get disbarred?"

"I'm afraid of hitting you in the liver and getting sprayed by bile," Mike says.

Patrick laughs. A staccato explosion. He covers his mouth.

"You think that's funny?" Klemmer says, looking at Patrick. "Listen to this. An executive gets arrested for tax fraud and he's sent to prison. His cell mate turns out to be this huge, massively muscled guy. That night the muscle guy says to the executive, *You want to be the husband or the wife?* The executive says, *I don't know what you're talking about.* The muscle guy says it again, a little louder, *You want to be the husband or the wife?* The executive says, *I don't want to play this game.* The guy says it again, real loud, *I said, You want to be the husband or the wife?* The executive thinks for a second and says, *I guess I'll be the husband. Good,* the muscle guy says. *Now get over here and suck your wife's dick.*"

Everyone laughs except Patrick. He drinks from the tequila

bottle, more carefully, making sure not to disrupt his sunglasses. I take the bottle from his hands and drink. I'm standing near the fridge. An alcohol skip. There and then there. The last time before I'd stopped drinking again, I was lying on the sidewalk, face exposed, eyes stinging from a blizzard's sideways snow, and all I saw was pavement and shoes walking by. A last straw that wasn't. I missed the drinking, the new-feeling nights, the everything's possible, the camera all on me, and I started again. I tip the tequila, drink more. My heart's racing the way it does before a fight I care about.

"Holy, Holy, Holyfield," I say.

Round five ends. Holyfield walks back to his stool, looking old, looking frustrated. When a fighter ages the last thing to go is his power but by then it usually doesn't matter. The old fighter is too slow, can't get his punches off, doesn't have the reflexes to block shots coming at him. There's a welt on Holyfield's forehead. When he spits out his mouthpiece red saliva drips down his chin. He breathes heavy.

"He looks like shit," Klemmer says.

"He still has his punch," I say.

"The old man's washed up."

"Tell us," Patrick says. "What do you mean by washed up?"

"You never heard that expression before?" Klemmer says. "They don't have that expression in Erin Go Bragh land?"

"Washed up," Steve says for Patrick. "It means he's finished."

"He's finished?"

"I'm just translating," Steve says.

"Forget it," Mike says.

"Tell us what they mean by washed up," Patrick says. "I don't like the sound of it."

"Forget it."

"Are they talking about Luz? About how she works in a laundry? Tell us what they mean."

"You're drunk," Mike says.

"I know what I am. We're all drunk. Maggoty drunk. Boys night out. This is what this is, right?"

The bottle of tequila is in his hands and he takes a drink.

"That's right," I say.

"That's right," Patrick repeats. "You think I'm washed up, then?"

"I don't really think about it," I say.

"You're thinking because I work as a janitor I'm washed up? I know the way you look at me. I knew this afternoon. You looked at my eye and you looked at me and you're thinking I'm a pufter."

"What do you care what I think?"

"Nothing for it now. I know about you too. Mike told me you fuck your students."

I lean forward, look at where Patrick's bad eye is behind his sunglasses.

"I like students," I say. "I like students and you like laundromat workers who beat the shit out of you."

"My fourth graders were a bit young, don't you think?"

"What's a pufter?" Klemmer says.

The bell rings. Holyfield stands. The second pulls the stool through the ropes. Holyfield moves forward, but his heart doesn't look in it.

"Who else did you tell?" I ask Mike.

"No one," he says.

"You didn't tell your wife?"

"She's my wife."

The referee stops the action, tells Holyfield's corner to clean up the water they've spilled.

"You're imagining I'm a pufter, then?" Patrick says.

"Watch the fight," I say. "Or I'll ship you to Vegas to mop up that mess."

Patrick laughs, keeps laughing, doesn't cover his mouth.

"I could," he says. "I'm quite handy with the mop. Quite handy."

He lifts the bottle of tequila. Mike grabs the bottle from him.

"No more for you," Mike says.

The corner wipes the canvas dry, and the referee signals time in. The two men walk to each other. Holyfield throws a looping left hook that misses. He throws another that misses again. He looks like an amateur and pays, gets hit with two fast jabs. Holyfield follows the kid around the ring, but he can't get close enough. The kid moves to the side and to the side again, keeps landing jabs.

"Kick her fecking ass," Patrick says to the TV.

"*Her* ass?" Klemmer says.

"Shut up," Mike says.

When the fight's over I'll tell them to leave. I'll dump the extra snacks, gather the empty bottles, go down alone. One of my students works as a hostess in a nearby restaurant. She's asked me to come by for a drink. I told her I'd wait until the semester was officially over, but my semesters end earlier and earlier each year.

Holyfield misses with another hook and the kid hits him hard and hard again. The second punch opens a gash over Holyfield's eye and Holyfield backs up, wipes his brow with his glove, looks at the blood. It's a deep cut in old skin. Holyfield blinks. Blinks again. Patrick is out of his seat. Blood fills Holyfield's eye. Patrick pulls back his arm and throws a punch at the TV. The image goes dark. The screen's dented. Patrick turns. He almost looks comfortable. We're all seated, all spectators. He takes off his sunglasses with the hand he hit the TV. All around his eye is purple, the eye almost completely closed, red where it should be white, a sliver of glossy pupil.

"Do you think I'm proud of this?" he says. "I'll go to work Monday morning and they'll all have a good laugh. They're always laughing. She laughs too. She laughs when I sneeze from her cats. She laughs when I'm tired from work. She calls me worthless and laughs. She laughs after she hits me."

"Hit her back next time," I say.

"I can't."

"What are you? You've got balls, don't you? You've got balls between your legs. You know how to make a fist. You just busted my fucking television. Hit her next time she hits you."

"I get lonely," he says.

"There's plenty of women out there," I say.

"Not for the likes of me. I get lonely and she knows it. If you haven't noticed, I'm not very social. If you haven't noticed, I don't get on well around people, especially women. When she hit me this morning, I told her that was the last straw. I didn't take the trash out right away and she hit me, and I told her that was the last straw. *That's the last straw, Luz*, I said. She only laughed."

Patrick puts on his sunglasses. He starts to laugh. His staccato laugh builds, but instead of ending abruptly it changes into sobbing and he cries like a child, not able to catch his breath. Mike stands and puts his hand on Patrick's shoulder and Patrick holds onto Mike, how I picture their walk through those dark woods. Steve and Jason don't move. Klemmer keeps his mouth shut. He hasn't been with a woman in two years.

"I'd laugh too," I say.

"No," Patrick says on an exhale.

"I would. After all the shit you've taken, all you do is tell her it's the last straw? I'd laugh my fucking head off."

Patrick lets go of Mike. He wipes at his snot-filled nose. The sleeve of his windbreaker glistens.

"Then you'd be as cruel as the bitch I live with," he says.

"You're the bitch. I wanted to see the end of this fucking fight. Holyfield has the heart to pull it out."

"He has no chance," Patrick says. "His heart is gone."

"You're wrong," I say.

"He's not the man he was," Patrick says. "He's getting washed up. He's getting old. He has to accept that. We all have to accept things."

"Fuck off."

"You too," Patrick says. "That's why you fuck your students. That's why you fuck everyone. Mike tells me you fuck everyone. He says you think you're a movie star. You think you're in a movie. He says you say that whenever you're drunk. You're not a movie star. You're a teacher. I was a teacher and you're a teacher. You're a fecking teacher who fucks his students."

I'm up. I'm charging. I slam Patrick against the wall, turn him around, lock his neck in my arm. I've got his pants. I'm pulling them down, pulling down his underwear. His balls are small and pink, hanging low like he's sick. I lift my hand and slap his balls as hard as I can. Patrick folds and I let go of his neck. He falls to the floor.

"Pussy," I say.

"Pussy," I say again, quiet.

Mike lifts Patrick and walks him to the bathroom to clean him up. The guys leave. The fight is over, at least on my big screen. If they hurry they'll be able to catch the last rounds at a sports bar. If the fight lasts. If Holyfield's cut stops bleeding. If Holyfield still has the heart, the balls. If not, they'll be able to watch the press conference with Holyfield sitting in front of a microphone, tinted sunglasses hiding his damage.

Mike and Patrick come out of the bathroom.

"We're going," Mike says.

I don't say anything.

"Tell us what I owe for the repair," Patrick says.

"Whatever."

"Tell us what I owe. I'll pay."

"Come on," Mike says.

"I think I'm going to puke," Patrick says.

They're out of my apartment before he does. I stay seated.

I hear someone retching on the street.

"Holy Holy Holyfield."

I throw a punch. Another. Pretend punches with no punches coming back.

The siren starts.

The truck's moving toward Eighth Avenue and the sound gets closer and takes over everything.

like forking toast at breakfast

He beat his father, said take off your glasses before I knock you out, spent time in juvie, fought men when he was a kid, said he boxed but didn't, his ring name Hammer Hand, laughs when I believe him, he's that big, fists that wide, Orange-County tough, tells stories of low-riders, of men blowing him for money, of breaking into Brando's house.

He's come to Manhattan like a *Midnight Cowboy* scene, movie before our time. They stop me on the street too, mostly older ones, ask if I'm Richard Gere, officer, gigolo, but really *Days of Heaven* kid (but I'm blond), and after another man uses the line (before he asks how much) I find the movie, watch.

We're going to be movie stars. We break into auditions without SAG cards, break into buildings just to take, just to use, he says, when a scene's about taking. He practices moves he'll use and I practice mine, like forking toast at breakfast when it's morning-after and they've made me breakfast and I've got my shirt off and I'm picking up toast with my fork.

Then I leave NYC (college). In Herter Hall's basement bathroom, stall doors removed, holes carved into side panels, men stand and sit and (look at me) tell me what they want and it's in their throats, that need-thickness. Then I return (graduated). Sometimes I take money.

Sometimes I take gifts. I get my SAG card doing an under-5 on *One Life to Live*. Then I quit. Too.

I work with him some days when he needs extra hands, spread flashing tar like frosting to fill holes, spread aluminum coating, and up here, closer to sky, to circling planes waiting, sometimes we find a ball, throw it, watch it arc to a faraway roof. Sometimes we smash a bottle just to hear. When the job's done we strip, wipe our elbows, forearms, hands with rags soaked in gasoline, shove our work clothes into Hefty bags, drive downtown where we live, different streets.

He drives back to California. To start again. Finds a place near Hollywood. Finds Jesus.

He's back in NYC for 2 weeks, stays in a hotel, touches the poor, asks to meet, tells me about Jesus, tells me about voices he hears. He's lost his humor, looks to heaven when he swears. He's stopped laughing. I tell him God wouldn't want that. We hug. He smiles not a smile. He still has his dimples, the most Hollywood part of him.

Sometimes we talk on the phone. He says he needs to start a church. He says he hears bad voices.

He moves his feet
off a branch
big body
dropping
and what's he hear when pressure presses ears, birds or wind or rope scraping bark (I've never listened in the San Gabriel Mountains) or just pressing, black dots (of no more oxygen coming in) expanding?

Sometimes when I'm drunk and no one's out I walk Central Park's cross-street at 96th, not a movie-move, screaming, carrying a rock, waiting to smash whatever comes. What, what, what, what, what did you do?

1 time in a bathroom in a bar, a bowl of fresh apples on a long marble sink like a still life, we started smashing—skin breaking, pulp exploding, cider smell everywhere—and left the bar laughing.

We'd wanted what Brando was. Did his voice, recited his speech from the back of the cab.

Some nights ended in Times Square. We watched the dancers. How their eyes went places we needed.

I still do sometimes. Fork my toast. Lift the piece up. Slow as I want. Look at me.

a picture of you

The phone lights up and it's Shayna. I'm at my desk, sitting, but when I hear her voice I get up and stand by the window so she can see me. My eyes aren't what they used to be, but they're close. I can see her bra. It's black. I can almost see her smirk, the dimple that forms when she's up to something, but that's more memory, less sight. If I need to go over there and see it, her dimple, her smile, her up-to-something, that part of Shayna and more, I just have to cross the street. She moves closer to her window.

"Show me some shin," she says.

I stick my leg out on the fire escape.

"Wait," she says. "Hold still."

Shayna disappears for a moment and returns.

"Don't say cheese," she says.

"I never say cheese."

I see the flash of her Polaroid go off. She's taken other Polaroid shots of me, up close, so close my face looks misshapen. She stays quiet as the photo develops.

"Done," she says.

"How'd it come out?"

"It has a little of my fire escape and then darkness. It's a picture of you, but you're not there."

"Just the essence of me."

"Exactly."

"You can't see me at all?"

"Not at all. Only I know you're there. Only I know it's a picture of you."

Shayna lives on the other side of Bedford Street, one building over, also on the third floor. Lucky three. High enough to kill yourself in a fall. Low enough to spit accurately at the drunken loudmouths stumbling from Chumley's at 3 a.m. I didn't know she lived across the street until she'd lived there a full year. I didn't know her except we'd met when she was twelve and I was twenty-two and then again twelve years later at my cousin's wedding, a whole extra lifetime for her. She'd been best friends with my cousin at twelve, a remnant friend at twenty-four. I was less than a remnant. I'd spoken to my cousin once in those twelve years and that was to congratulate her at her wedding in Richmond before I returned to my assigned table and finished my double bourbon. Sitting across from me had been Shayna. We said hello, checked each other out, but she left before the main course was cleared. I stayed through the cake cutting, had danced with another friend of my cousin's, a current friend, who spent the night in my hotel room. A year later Shayna and I met on Bedford Street, did a double-take, and started to talk. I kissed Shayna's cheek when we said goodbye.

"It's quiet tonight," I say, looking out the window.

"It's early," she says. "Did you hear the new tour guide? I could have sworn he put on an English accent when he said the word *speak-easy*."

"I heard him."

"He spoke for way too long. That speakeasy is the bane of our existence."

I see Shayna's head tilt. I can't tell if she's looking at her fire escape or perusing my side of the street.

"One day we'll blow up Chumley's," I say. "One day we'll put all the tour guides out of business."

"A man with a plan. Where will they take the tourists if not to Manhattan's most fraudulent bar?"

"The Empire State Building. Keep it cliché. Keep it simple."

"You go, B-Da."

Shayna has taken to calling me B-Da after I called myself B-Da after I told her the story of B-Da. Family friends, closer than the Richmond cousins but not much, had a daughter. That daughter married a woman and the two of them had a son through artificial insemination. One day, the woman decided she wanted to be a man. She took hormones. She grew a light beard. She developed muscles. She had skin removed from her forearm to make something resembling a penis. The son had called them Mommy and Mommy. But the woman that was now a man wanted something new, something more creative. They came up with B-Da. Short for Butch Dad. B-Da was the word the son started using. The son was only two years old. I fast-forwarded the son's life to third grade, saw him crying in the playground as kids taunted him for having a B-Da. I fast-forwarded some more, saw him breaking down during therapy. It didn't matter how much we'd progressed. Kids were kids and kids were brutal and brutal was how they'd treat B-Da's kid. The night I told Shayna the story of B-Da, I'd been feeling lost. I took the fez Shayna kept on her bookshelf, one of Shayna's many thrift shop purchases, put the fez on my head, and said I felt something had switched off in me lately, like I was me but not me. I said I felt like a B-Da. Shayna had smirked. The nickname stuck.

"So, B-Da. What's going on?"

"B-Da is reading stories and correcting papers," I say.

"Poor B-Da. How can I help?"

"You want to correct some?"

"Sure. Bring a batch over."

172

And that's that. Like always. She throws out the invitation and I say I'll be right there and all I have to do is cross the street. It's like a game. It is a game.

"Do you want some ice cream?" I say.

"I could go for some ice cream."

Shayna waves and I end the call.

I brush my teeth. Pull my hand through my hair. Put on jeans and a fresh T. Go down. Walk to the corner store and look at the ice cream selections. I pick one with swirls of fudge and marshmallow and different nuts. The more in it, the better. Shayna likes her junk. She's not a Manhattan neurotic who obsesses about food choices. Shayna is tall and thin. She's almost as tall as I am and when she wears heels we look eyes to eyes, kiss lips to lips. But she's dark haired and I'm blond. She's twenty-five and I'm thirty-five. I pay the cashier. He looks tired.

Shayna buzzes me up and I hand her the ice cream, kiss her, lift her off the floor even though she says she hates that, press her against the wall, a pretend-passion move like this is a movie, and let her down. She takes a fork from her utensil drawer, the left drawer, and puts the fork in the ice cream. When the fork tilts the ice cream will be ready. Forks work better than spoons. It's an ice cream-eating detail I've taught her. What Shayna has taught me is far more important. I don't even know the full lesson, can't write it down in a thesis statement or explain it precisely in a structured body paragraph like I make my students do in comp class, but Shayna interprets my dreams beautifully and she calms me when I feel especially lost, taking my hand in hers and pressing my palm with her fingers just right as if that touch, that pressure, will remind me I'm here. I have a sort-of girlfriend, so Shayna is the other woman, the girl across the street. She's been good about that. When I show up drunk at her door, she lets me in and actually enjoys me, laughs at most of the things I do when I'm drunk, like announcing I'll take my shirt off before taking it off, like making her feel my muscles, like repeating things in threes, which I didn't know I did until Shayna told me.

"What's cooking, B-Da?"

"I'm getting sick of my place," I say.

"Why is that?"

"The only good thing is the window across from yours."

"That is a good thing."

"They started putting in new stairs. There's splintered wood all over the fucking place and plaster dust. There's a film of dust covering everything."

"But soon you'll have new stairs."

"I liked the old stairs."

"Maybe you'll like the new ones better."

The fork tips. The ice cream's ready. Shayna digs in and gives me the first forkful, full of marshmallow and fudge. She takes a forkful for herself and says, Yummmm before the ice cream could have hit her buds. Her enthusiasm is sometimes a cover, but it's a better cover than cursing the world. I'm tired of my life, more and more tired. I'm too old to be Manhattan poor and too set to look for higher-paying work that would suck forty-plus hours a week from how I live, from doing what I do and how I do it. Too set and too tired and non-stop, that's where I'm most tired, the non-stop drinking, the non-stop going out, but I'm too tired to stop even that.

"Did you bring papers?" Shayna says.

"I didn't."

"Why not?"

"There will be others."

We go into her bedroom and eat ice cream. It's air conditioned in her bedroom and I sometimes joke but not really how I only see

174

women with air conditioners and kitchens since my tiny studio has neither, only a fan and a hot plate. There's a girl in my evening class who sits in the front row, holds my eyes, sticks around to talk after the other students have left. She's very pretty and could have any boy in the class, but when the teacher is B-Da the other boys have no chance. I've asked her pointed questions and she's given the right answers. She has her own apartment with a kitchen and an air conditioner. Summer session ends the third week in July.

On Shayna's TV, something else I don't have, they're showing reruns of *The Sopranos*. Tony Soprano, everybody's favorite gangster slash sweetheart, is having a panic attack outside his own house.

"Tough guy," I say.

"He's not happy," Shayna says.

"He's happy enough."

"Then why is he freaking out?"

"He just is."

"Nothing just is. He's not happy with his life."

"He has his own code," I say. "He does what he does. Maybe he's as content as he can be."

"He's about to pass out."

"Look at the size of his house."

"And?"

"I'm not saying a big house means contentment. I'm not saying that."

Shayna smirks.

"I'm not," I say.

"That was three *I'm nots* and you're not even drunk."

"Let's get a drink."

"A drink."

"Let's go drinking."

She takes a forkful of ice cream. She doesn't swallow right away. I can almost see the swirls melting against her tongue.

"Let's," I say. "A gin and tonic for a hot summer night sounds even better than Ben and Jerry's."

"Are you sure?"

"Come on."

"Fine. Okay. Fine."

"That was two *Fines*."

"I guess it was."

Shayna puts on flip-flops, red ones that highlight her red-painted toes. She takes her bag, a Fendi knockoff. We walk down her good stairs and we're out the door. I look around. My sort-of girlfriend lives in the neighborhood and I don't want to get caught. She's probably at the gym, running on the treadmill, keeping her body fit for the corporate suits she wears to her corporate job. I've been seeing her for two years. I've been cheating on her for two years.

"Where to, B-Da?"

"This way," I say.

We walk the Village streets. There's a bar I haven't gone to in a while, a decent place with a long wood bar and not so packed with kids we'll need to scream. There are plenty of barstools and we take two at the far end. I order a gin and tonic for Shayna and a bourbon rocks for me. The bartender breaks my twenty and returns less change than I'd expected. It's a rich city. Teaching hardly pays my rent.

"I got kicked out of here once," I say.

"How come?"

"I was drunk."

"People go to bars to get drunk."

"I was out-of-control drunk. I broke a mirror in the bathroom with my fist and didn't even cut myself. I didn't even bleed."

"Why doesn't that surprise me? Does the bartender recognize you?"

"I don't recognize him."

"You were drunk."

"I wasn't blind."

"Are you sure, B-Da?"

I drink my bourbon. She drinks her gin. I look straight at her.

"I am."

"Are you staring me down now?"

"I'm just staring," I say.

"Good."

"Good."

"Good. There. Three times."

"We're not drunk yet," I say.

"Not blind drunk."

"Not yet."

"I'm never blind, B-Da," Shayna says.

I order two more drinks. I don't think the bartender's the one who kicked me out. I could have taken that one. I can take this one. After I was thrown out, I went to another bar and another and time skipped and I was face down on the street, getting up, looking at myself in a storefront window, the night making it a mirror, and my eye was swollen shut. I didn't remember getting in a fight. I didn't remember falling. When I taught the next day, eye dark purple, forehead bruised, my students wondered what else I did besides reading their work.

We drink our second drinks and I order another round.

"I'm already high," Shayna says.

"Get higher."

"I didn't eat tonight."

"We had ice cream."

"You're right. We did."

The bartender sets down the drinks, breaks my twenty.

"You have small wrists," she says.

"I think you've made a comment about every part of my body."

"Here's looking at you, B-Da," she says. "I like looking at you. You have a beautiful body."

"Thanks."

"Elegant wrists. Is that better? I could put my hands around them."

She takes my wrist in her hand and holds it, her red nails touching, thumb and middle finger.

"See?" she says.

"You have big hands."

"Not as big as yours," Shayna says. "You know what they say about big hands."

"Tell me."

"They need big gloves."

Shayna lets go of my wrist.

"You seem distracted tonight," she says. "What's wrong? Thinking about your girlfriend?"

"I'm here with you so I'm thinking about you. I do think about you."

"That's sweet, B-Da."

"I do."

"I can take care of myself."

"I wasn't being condescending."

"It sounded that way."

"Whatever," I say, and it comes out tired.

A group of four women walk into the bar. They're dressed downtown-chic and they've perfected that far-away stare where their eyes never fully connect as they glance over the room. I play the same game. I look past them, past the door, onto the street. A cab drives by too fast, the light on, the driver looking for a fare.

"Anyone interesting?"

"Not as interesting as you. That's not condescending either."

"Whatever," she says.

I drink my drink, ahead of Shayna now. She's hardly touched hers, but I order another round. The four women have arranged themselves on the barstools near the door. I'm not looking directly at them. I'm looking at the bartender's hand, the angle of the bottle while he pours my drink, making sure it's a generous pour. It's not generous enough. He takes my money.

"Are you shooting for blind?" Shayna says.

"Maybe. Maybe I am shooting for blind. Which means I'm not blind."

"In some ways. In some ways you're very in touch with yourself."

"And you're the wisest woman I know. *Know thyself.* You know what that's from?"

"That was three *knows*, but who's counting? What's it from?"

"The Delphic oracle. *Know thyself* and *Nothing in excess.* Those were the words written at the oracle."

"One out of two ain't bad."

"Cheers," I say and drink.

"I have a mean idea," I say. "Let's call Stephanie later."

Stephanie is my cousin from Richmond. Stephanie is Shayna's friend from childhood. Stephanie was there when Shayna and I first met, when Shayna was twelve and I was twenty-two. Stephanie is married to a man Shayna wouldn't look at let alone marry. Shayna's dream is to be a mother one day, and I already know she'll be a good mother.

She'll be warm and patient and she'll hold her kid's hand and press the right places to make her kid calm like she presses my palm. The first night I spent in her bed, Shayna showed me a book she'd just bought on kanji, the characters that stand for Japanese words. Each character was a picture that could be interpreted. We'd drawn our own kanji on each other's backs. In the morning I rubbed three straight lines across Shayna's ass. She asked what the word was, and I said, Pancakes. A stack of three pancakes. Shayna made three pancakes for each of us that morning and I knew she'd be the kind of mother to make her kid pancakes before her kid went off to school. I didn't know if my cousin Stephanie would make pancakes for her kid, but I did know Stephanie would never read about kanji and that her husband would never draw lines across her skin. Weddings always depressed me. Stephanie's wedding did worse. Standing foolishly at the altar, they'd looked like two college buddies, passionless.

"I want to call Stephanie and tell her I'm in your bed," I say.

"I don't think that would make her happy."

"It would shake up her life a little. Shake up her little life."

"When we were growing up, she always talked about her big cousin in New York City."

"She wanted to fuck me."

"Don't we all."

"Now all she fucks is that zero she married."

"Her husband is very nice," Shayna says. "I'm sure he's very good to her."

"Good. Nice. Pleasant. Agreeable. I'd rather be very hated than called very nice."

"Know thyself."

"I do."

"Sometimes."

"I just don't think."

"You think more than anyone I know."

"You're wrong. I just do. That's my salvation."

"No. You think. I see how much you think. You can play it cool, but you're thinking all the time."

"I'm not thinking now," I say.

"Drink up, B-Da."

"You drink up. I'm way ahead of you. Way ahead of you."

"I know where I stand," she says.

We're eyes to eyes. Her mouth looks hurt and I'm thinking I don't want to hurt her, I hurt everyone and don't want to hurt her, and I think how I'm thinking and try to stop and I keep looking at her eyes.

"I know," she says.

I don't have to ask what she knows.

"It's a competition," I say.

"It's always a competition with you."

"This is a real competition. This one could have stakes. Who will break first? Who will say *I love you* first?"

"Is that right?"

"It is right."

Shayna blinks once and keeps looking. I can keep my eyes on hers the whole night if she wants, all night if I have to. I lift my drink and keep my eyes where they are and drink and put my glass down.

"A competition with stakes," she says.

"That's what it's becoming. We can look at each other like we're looking now. We fuck like we fuck. We stay in bed until morning, which is something we don't do with anyone else, not the people we pick up."

"And when you're done sleeping over you take that short walk of shame across Bedford Street."

"It's not shameful."

"It's not pure."

"Pure," I say and don't say anything else. The word hangs there then disappears.

"Who?" I say. "Who will break first and say it?"

She's holding my eyes. Her eyes are usually lit, lit for me, light, but they're not. I can sort of see her mouth, serious, no playful smirk at all. There's a space between her lips. A small space.

"You've never said it, have you?" she says.

"Are you sure?"

"I'm pretty sure."

"I've said it in kanji."

"No. And that wouldn't count. You've never really said it."

"Not with feeling."

"Me neither," she says. "I would rather be alone than waste my time pretending. When this gets too much I'll walk."

"Is it too much?"

"It's getting there," she says.

"What's the kanji sign for love?" I say, trying to get back to light, trying to keep it from getting too-much. When the other woman, whatever other woman I'm seeing, feels too much, I'm the one who walks.

"I don't know the kanji sign for love," Shayna says. "I only know the signs of love."

"Love," I say, and the word comes out like it always comes out when I say it.

"Love, love," I say.

"Three times," she says.

"Three lines for pancakes."

Shayna's eyes are still on mine. Her lips are closer together, the slightest space.

"I love my kanji," I say.

"They're only symbols," she says.

"I know."

"I know you know," she says.

I finish my drink and put another twenty on the bar, the last twenty in my wallet.

"I wonder," I say. "I wonder if B-Da ever says *I love you.* The real B-Da. I wonder if the real B-Da, the one with the new beard and muscles, if he or they ever says it to his or their wife. I'm sure B-Da says it to the kid. The kid is the reason B-Da is B-Da. But do you think B-Da ever says it to the wife? With feeling?"

"You tell me, B-Da."

"Maybe B-Da used to. Before B-Da became B-Da."

Shayna turns and reaches into her bag. She puts the Polaroid flat on the bar. It's the one she took tonight, from her window, of me. It's the one of me but not me. It's almost all darkness, the outline of her fire escape and then dark. If I didn't know the camera was pointed in my direction when she took the shot, I'd never know I was there, somewhere.

Shayna picks up her bag and stands.

ten

She's doing the same thing I'm doing, sort of.

After rapid back-and-forth messages (biography questions and answers, banter to prove we can banter), she tells me she's studying writing. I tell her I teach writing. Her photos are selfies. In one, she's standing in front of a mirror wearing a summer skirt that shows off thin, strong legs. Her face is smudged by the indoor flash. My photo is a book jacket photo of me looking starving-artist moody.

She finally admits it. She set up a profile on OkCupid to get material for her assignment. She's taking a Lyrical Essay course and hopes to collect as many messages as possible and create a verbal collage. I send her a question. *What exactly is a lyrical essay?* She writes back, *I don't fully know*. I tell her I like Hemingway, Spartan and simple, and she tells me she likes Joyce and David Foster Wallace and Claudia Rankine and Jean Toomer and plenty of others in between, which makes her, she assumes, less lyrically challenged. I ask how her lyrical essay is coming along. She says she's received too many responses. She asks why I chose her profile beyond the obvious. I tell her I'm writing a story of my own. *About the thrills of Internet dating?* she writes. *Thrilled to meet you*, I write back. I leave the rest out—that I plan to bed ten different women from the site in ten days. I'm from the write-what-you-know school of fiction. I live it, then tweak it, shaping reality into story.

The only time I write lyrically is when I send emails to Jay Schlager, a college friend and fellow writer whose ability to compose raunchy limericks, haikus, mini-parodies, and short paragraphs of mocking-mean that, alliteratively-lyrically, match mine. We build on each other's emails, pushing the irreverence, multiplying the filth. And why not? We're writers, but we're also straight and White and American and male and, White fragility aside, the publishing business has shunned us because our straight, White, American, male stories are no longer, like the expression, in vogue. So we write to each other as a joke, as a way to laugh off our venom, impotently asserting the very power that's rendered us impotent in the real publishing world.

Recently we've made the most ungentlemanly gentleman's bet. I say I can do it. Jay says I can't. I tell him I'll write a story about it. He tells me I'll be viewed as a sexist and sexism, he reminds me, even playful, is a tough sell these days, especially in the litmag world. I tell him that will be part of my challenge.

Ten women.

Ten days.

One story.

For nine days I've been sending messages and getting responses, and I've registered nine notches on my proverbial belt. I haven't been sleeping much. The only writing I've done is on OkCupid. It takes time to woo women, meet them in person, woo them some more, usually with drinks, and finally, finally!, close the deal. I'm on schedule. I have until midnight to reach number ten and then I'll start my story.

The lyrical-essay woman and I shoot messages back and forth until, inevitably, the way it happened with the nine before, none of them writers but all possessing vaginas, number ten sends her name and number. I add Natalie to my Contacts, followed by an O for OkCupid. When I scroll down names on drunken nights, buzzed close to blackout, I imagine each woman and what she looks like naked and what she's like in bed and what I want at that moment, always at-that-moment when I'm drunk, one woman's name falling into the next, and it's almost playful, almost joyful, as close to lyrical as I'll ever get, and maybe I'll tell Natalie about my found-poem/list-poem phone-contacts when I see her, after I move in for the first kiss, after I take her to her bed or my bed, after I close the deal on number ten so I can write what I know.

   Ten. It's a story about a bet. It's a story about a man too old for bets, not a college kid anymore, not a young man new to the city and ready to conquer, but a man with a job and perspective and history, bored from responsibility, scared of what tenure means, a lifelong job so safe, so secure, it will be his last job, ever, before he retires and dies. I've told Jay about my fucking but not my fear. Our poems and parodies are game, but the fear of never connecting, of fucking around until I'm too old to fuck, of teaching until I'm too old to teach, of never finding another publisher or a woman to love, a place to house my writing and a place to house me, beyond that warm smooth slit between legs, is never in my words to Jay Schlager.

   At the end of the week, our department is moving into a new building. Last week, a man came around with boxes and labels. I assembled the first box, filled it with books to see how many a box could hold. It took so little time, I filled a second box and a third and suddenly the shelves were empty. It was true. I could pack up my life, at least my professional life, in an hour. If I burned the boxes I could move on, me and whatever I could fit in my pockets.

   Two of the books I packed were my books. The rest of the books weren't. They were the books I liked to read, the books I taught, and a few how-to-write-fiction books that were crap, but when an interested student wanted exercises on plot or character, I'd hand over a review copy like a gift. There were several thick anthologies containing identical stories, some solid, some almost too teachable, and some too lyrical for me, though I'd never used the word lyrical. I wasn't sure how much shelf space our new offices had, but I knew the rooms would be smaller by a few square feet, so I chucked a few anthologies into the giant trashcans they'd put in the hall and heard the weight of pages hitting plastic. I could have stacked the anthologies outside my door for curious students to pick up and read, but in the margins of the stories I hated I wrote small notes, vulgar and critical. These notes for myself made it easier for me to read the stories I was supposed to read, so I could speak about them to colleagues I was supposed to speak to, colleagues whose tastes were anti-Spartan, who used words like peda-gogical and tautological, who talked about outcomes assessments and spot teaching and peer-centered environments, who carried their books to class in professorial leather briefcases or strapped onto little strollers like old people carting their day's groceries home, wheels squeaking. I'd never get that kind of old.

I'm going to call you, I write.

Half a minute later she writes back, *Good. But I need to finish my assignment.*

I hit Contacts. I hit Natalie. She picks up.

"So when's it due?" I say.

"It's due tomorrow. I've narrowed down the messages and the parts of messages I want to use, but the way I've ordered them feels off. I want a more subtle throughline to emerge. I also need to work in some repeated beats and words. My professor broke down how repetitions create lyrical sounds in a mathematical way. When I read aloud what I've assembled so far, my essay doesn't sound very musical."

Her voice is raspy, but not like she's trying for sexy. It's the voice of a woman who's just finished screaming, whose vocal cords are so raw she can only speak quietly, and I like it.

"Tell me what kind of throughline you're looking for, or what kind of repetitions you need. I'll write the message, hit Send, and your lyrical essay will fall lyrically into place."

"That wouldn't be honest," she says.

"Most writing isn't honest."

"The process wouldn't be honest."

"You're taking this assignment seriously."

"Don't you take your writing seriously?"

"I used to."

"And now?"

"Now I don't write much."

"Why not?"

"My books didn't sell. So it's tough to sell a new book."

"The publishing Catch-22. I've heard about that."

"It's brutal out there. Besides, I've run out of subjects."

"I thought you were writing a new story about OkCupid."

"Not a lyrical story."

"Well," she says, and I wait.

"Well, I'm forcing myself to take this assignment seriously," she says. "If I told you what to write and you wrote it and sent it to me and I used it, that wouldn't be true to the assignment. We're supposed to incorporate found words and build our own words around them. My professor made it very clear we should manipulate as little as possible except for sound. He said assembling words is very different from directing words."

"Writing is all about directing words," I say.

"You obviously don't teach the lyrical essay in your class," she says, and she laughs a strange laugh, each exhale separate from the last, and raspy too.

"I'll never teach the lyrical essay. And I'll never write a lyrical essay."

"Never say never," she says.

"*Sag Niemals Nie.*"

"You speak German?"

"No. When I was in Germany, they were showing James Bond's *Never Say Never Again*, and I memorized the title. I've seen all the Bond movies. They don't pretend they're more than movies and when Bond ages out, they stick a new one in. Only Sean Connery came back after he said he'd never be Bond again. If I send you an email about *Sag Niemals Nie*, you can use the German *Nevers*. You can even try to make them sound musical. Yours would be the sole lyrically-bi-lingual essay in the class."

"I doubt it," she says, and then there's quiet on the line.

And outside it's quiet too, a rare city time when not one car goes by, not one horn honks, not one person shouts, not a siren, not a single pigeon's coo. I walk over to the window and look three stories down to the street and there's no one.

"Are you there?" she says.

"I am. We should meet."

"When?"

"Right now. Carpe diem. Where are you?"

"Upper West. Near Columbia. Grad housing."

"I can be there in forty minutes."

"I didn't shower yet. And I have my essay to write."

"Forty-five minutes. The Abbey Pub. On 105th, just east of Broadway. You know what I look like, only I'm not black and white."

"Too bad," she says.

"I'll wear a white T-shirt."

"It's freezing out."

"That's how tough I am," I say. "White T-shirt. Abbey Pub. Forty-five minutes. See you there."

I've done my push-ups and sit-ups, so I'm a little salty, a little sweaty. I wash my underarms in the sink, brush my teeth, look myself over. In the commercials they call it a touch of gray, but with my hair almost crew-cut short the gray blends with the blond and unless I'm smiling, I look fifteen years younger than I am.

If there's one New York City bar I can call my regular, it's the Abbey. They have a beer and shot special, so it's a good place to start a heavy night of drinking. One of the waitresses was once my student. She'll ask how classes are going and I'll tell her what's new at the college and she'll nod at the bartender to fill my glass at least once a night. I never act up in the Abbey. I've been kicked out of too many bars and this place, sort of old, sort of dark, a little below street level, its clientele a mix of happy students and morbid drunks, feels like in-between.

The bartender comes over, says hello, familiarly, but not so familiar he puts down my shot and beer before I'm through the door. My ex-student is nowhere around. Natalie isn't here either. One of the regulars sits on the stool closest to the door, drinking her carafe of red and reading the *Times*. There's a young guy, Guinness in his hand, head tilted toward the TV, watching hockey. The Rangers goalie blocks a shot and play stops. I order the special, a Maker's rocks and whatever beer of the day they're giving out. The bartender pops the cap and puts down a bottle of PBR. It's one of the beers men drank where I grew up, when I grew up. The bartender pours the Maker's.

Ten. A story about a bet. My idea is that by winning the bet, by bedding ten women in ten days, a pretty good feat at any age, the protagonist will assert his youth and trump his tenure, turning it from a symbolic death sentence to a recognition there's plenty of life to live. A gig that can never be taken away becomes freeing, not suffocating. There's the joy of having no pressure to prove. There's the steady income for drinking and everything else. After fucking ten women in ten days, the professor will know, truly know, he's still virile, still attractive, still has what it takes. I already know the story's last scene. I've written down the details, directed them with such control the scene's already closer to real-memory than invented-moment. And I've lived part of that scene, the walking away part, hundreds of times. The professor leaves the tenth woman's apartment, winner of a gentleman's bet, goes directly to his new office, with its bare shelves and polished floor, and starts to write with renewed energy, his fingers pressing the keyboard, not Hollywood-smashing but real, the lines coming, the pacing, the arc, the subtext making less more, touching the gut like when he was a real writer, his first book out, a signed contract for the second, no question about a third, a fourth. A job for life. A lust for life. It's a loose connection but a connection. Ten. Tenure. The title in the conflict. The conflict in the number.

The door opens and by reflex I check. Her posture is dancer-straight. Her face, no longer smudged by flash, is beautiful, and only a small, raised scar at the top of her cheek breaks her symmetrical beauty. I've slept with seventeen Black women. Sometimes, when I can't sleep, I count.

"You should be ashamed luring me away from my desk on a school day," she says, and her voice, like on the phone, is raw.

"Maybe, but I'm not."

Natalie smiles. She takes off her coat, drapes it over the bar stool, and sits.

"What are you drinking?" I say.

"What are you drinking?"

"Bourbon. Maker's. And a beer."

"I normally don't drink whiskey."

"Try it," I say and hand her the glass.

She lifts the glass, takes a full sip, her face scrunches, turns happy, surprised. "It's very good. I'll have one too."

"Do you want a beer?"

"No thank you. I don't like beer."

I order another Maker's from the bartender. I force myself not to drink down mine for another. I don't want Natalie thinking I'm a full-fledged drunk, not yet anyway.

"I received twenty-three more messages," she says. "None of them worth using."

"You're getting a lot of play from your profile."

"It's because of the line I wrote at the end."

"What was it?"

"You don't remember? How many of these profiles do you respond to?" she says, raspy. Then she smiles. Her teeth are a little crooked, but her mouth's still great.

I smile back. "I respond to dozens. Actually, hundreds."

"*Looking for spontaneity with spontaneous people who know carpe diem's not the fish of the day.*"

"*Fish of the day*. Now I remember. I remembered the *carpe diem*."

"I thought it held the right note for a lyrical essay. Plus, it's sort of a signal for all the men out there to think I'm easy. I wanted to optimize my number of responses."

"*Euphemism*. You can title your essay *Euphemism*."

"That's a little stiff."

"Do all parts of the lyrical essay have to be lyrical?"

"To tell you the truth, I still don't know."

She's a fast drinker. Her glass is empty, and I order two more Maker's. I watch the bartender pour, count the alcohol going in. I'm enough of a regular that he uses a heavy hand.

192

"Can I ask you a clichéd question?" she says.

"Go ahead."

"Do you do this often? I mean honestly. Do you go on OkCupid and search for random women all the time?"

"Not random women. Spontaneous women."

"Okay, spontaneous women."

"I was bored, so I checked out the site. Some of the profiles are funny and I'm guessing a lot of them are fakes. I thought a few random meetings might give me material. Sort of what you're doing. So no, I don't do this often. I prefer meeting women in bars. Your post was well-written, I remember that, so I was curious. I figured maybe you'd say some memorable lines."

"Here I thought I was using you."

"We can use each other."

"Is that a euphemism too?" she says.

"No. When I write, the word usually means what the word means. I always think about subtext, but that's different. I don't hide behind euphemisms."

"I forgot. You're a Hemingway fan and a tough guy. Nice T-shirt, by the way."

I flex my arm for her. It's what I do when I drink. I flex my arms for women, ask them to feel my muscles, ask them to punch my stomach to feel my abs, all subtext for feel my cock, which they inevitably do at the end of the night. My rocks glass is empty. I don't ask Natalie to feel my arm. I order another round and she downs the rest of her Maker's.

"What's your story going to be about?" she says.

"A professor."

"Like you."

"Like me. And he meets a woman on OkCupid."

"Like me."

"We'll see how this goes. I have to see if you're character-worthy."

Natalie laughs her strange laugh.

"I never thought of myself that way," she says. "I don't know if I'd make a very good character."

"Do you make a very good person?"

"I don't know about very good."

"That's a good answer. It makes you a more layered character."

"I don't know if I'd make much of any kind of character, especially in a story with lots of dialogue. I'm usually quiet."

"You'll talk when you have to. Or you won't."

"Or I won't," she says.

Natalie lifts her drink and takes a long sip. She closes her eyes to taste the whiskey and I watch her swallow, watch the burn in her throat. Her mouth purses, relaxes. No artifice. No protection. Like she doesn't care, but in the what-others-think way, not the fuck-everything, fake-apathy way. She puts the glass down. She looks back at me. It's what I tell my students to do in their stories. Let the character do something and then let the character do something else. It's why I hate the word *as*.

"There aren't enough quiet people," I say. "Most people champ at the bit to enter every conversation. You can see them listening, but what they're really doing is waiting for the opening to tell you what they did or thought or felt or who they knew."

"Isn't that what conversation is? A sharing of ideas and experiences?"

"People want to spout, not share. It's all ego. But I'm a cynical man."

"Are you a good writer?"

"I have two novels published."

"That's not what I asked."

I could lift my drink, drink, pause, feign modesty or arrogance to set up a dramatic delivery. And that's the problem. I'm aware of everything. My camera's always on me, so everything feels posed.

"I used to be," I say.

"That's what you said on the phone."

"I'm consistent."

"People in my classes hate me," she says. "Everyone sugar-coats everything and it gets frustrating. It's college and it's expensive and they're supposed to be serious. Half the students can't write and half of them have nothing to write about. I hate to think I was like that when I was their age. The professors are constantly playing mediator and smooth out every critical comment before things get too honest. It's their job, I suppose, but I can't stomach their fear. In my creative writing classes, if something is shit, I say so."

"Good."

"You wouldn't think it was good if I were in your class."

"I would. I'd enjoy it. You'd say everything I was saying, but you'd say it harshly. When I was a student, I had a writing teacher who, if something was shit, he'd hold up the story by its corner, like he'd contaminate himself if he touched the whole page, and he'd walk over to the offending student and drop the story on their desk without a word."

"That's the teacher I'm looking for."

"He's dead."

The door opens and five college kids come in, loud and red-faced from the cold. Three girls, one pretty, two boys, one handsome. When they take one of the big booths, the pretty girl and handsome boy sit next to each other, which is how it will always be, smart or not, good writer or not. Ten would be easy for him too.

"We're both here for our writing," she says. "That makes me feel less guilty about drinking on a Monday afternoon."

"You should never feel guilty about drinking on a Monday afternoon."

"You obviously have only yourself to worry about."

"Who else are you worrying about?"

"My daughter. I didn't mention her in my post. I thought that might ruin the whole spontaneity thing."

"A conscious choice of omission. How old?"

"She's eleven."

"Is she a good kid?"

"She's a difficult kid."

"That's not what I asked," I say, and she misses it and I smile and she gets it.

"She's too difficult to be good. Plus, I'm a very single mom with questionable parenting skills, I'm afraid. My husband was a bad boy, which I liked, who turned out to be a bad man, which I didn't like. That's not a euphemism. It's more a cliché. He's locked up. It's me and my child."

"That can't be easy."

"It isn't."

"Write a memoir. Single mother. Difficult daughter. Husband locked up. You'll sell it in no time."

"I don't like my current life. I don't want to write about it. Not while I'm living it."

I raise the glass. "To easier times."

"Sorry. I told myself I wouldn't mention her. I wanted to pretend I was a free woman able to have a drink on a Monday afternoon with a handsome man."

"You're here. You're free right now."

"Until five. She's in the after-school program. I meet her at the bus stop."

I have to fuck ten women in ten days. At midnight the ten days are up. Jay emailed me this morning.

A writer whose psyche was frail
was relegated to bets about tail.
If he'd just been born other,
the offers—sweet smother!
But his male cock ensured he would fail.

I'd write Jay back when I'd won.

I'm a professor. She's a student. Not a kid student. She must be close to thirty, and I look at her eyes, wide-set, a little tired, a little far away, and the way alcohol does, magnifying everything, her eyes, my muscles, the need to win this bet, I see right through her, see her weariness, her past, her bad husband, her difficult kid, the schoolwork she needs to complete, an older college student years behind. And I see myself inside her. It will be that easy.

"Now," I say.

"Now?"

"You met me. You have two hours before your daughter's back. We both need to write. Take me home now."

She looks at me, looks at me.

"Okay," she says. "Let's go."

I leave the bills on the bar, leave the half-finished bottle of Pabst next to the empty rocks glasses. Natalie puts on her coat. I put on mine.

We're out of the Abbey.

We're crossing Broadway.

We're on Claremont Avenue.

We're in front of her building. She's turning the key. We're walking up stairs. We're in her apartment.

I've done this for so long. I once saw the great boxing champion Roberto Duran running in Central Park. He was too old to be fighting, too fat to be fighting, thirty pounds past his prime, but he was running around the loop. I passed him, saw it was him, turned back and ran next to him for a few strides, raising my own fists in recognition. Roberto Duran. Manos de Piedra. Hands of Stone. One of the greatest fighters of all time. Duran was breathing too hard, struggling, and it was clear he was training for a fight he wasn't ready to fight. But three weeks later I read he'd gone ten rounds with a young man and won. Roberto Duran was so comfortable in the ring, so at home, his breathing must have come easy. That's me bedding women. I have her bra off with a flick of the clasp. I have her jeans off. I spread her before me. She has close, dark hair and a beautiful cunt and I open her with my fingers. And like most women, no matter what they say, she lets me fuck her without a condom. And as soon as the head of my cock is in, then the shaft, one long stroke, it's official. I have my ten. I've won the bet. I could pull out and email Jay and brag about my bullshit macho prowess, which we'll write about, as limericks, as haikus, as back-and-forth emails, without any true feelings under the words, the worst kind of writing. I fuck her and fuck her, talking, telling, simple declarative sentences, and when she says she can't come any more I make her come one more time. And when she's done, I take out my cock, put it in her hand, and watch her jerk me off. The come comes out and so does any interest I have in anything.

I stand up. I put on my pants. I look around her room. On the dresser are framed photos of a girl with wide-set eyes and an up-to-something smile. I can see this kid causing trouble, so much trouble a screaming voice becomes hoarse. I look at the woman on the bed and there's no smile, no sparkle in her eyes, nothing lyrical at all.

"Ten," I say.

"Ten what?"

"Ten women. That's what I'm writing about. I needed to fuck ten women in ten days from OkCupid. The site's got the right name for a story. I made a bet."

"A bet?"

"It wasn't for money. It was for me. I'll write the story and something, the part around the story, whatever I need to say, will come. I need to live it, live some of it, to write it. I think that's the opposite of lyrical. I can't make up stories, not really, not the plots. I'm not even a good storyteller. At parties, or at dinners, I can deliver lines, I can counter-punch, but I don't tell stories. Telling stories isn't writing them, but the writers I know all tell stories and they talk in full, descriptive paragraphs, and most of them try so fucking hard."

"Well," she says and gets off the bed.

I watch her put on her underwear, more man's brief than woman's lingerie. I watch her put on her jeans, pointing her toes, slipping one leg in, slipping the other leg in. There's something kid-like in the way she dresses. She must have been a kid when she had a kid. She must have been too young to admit her husband, a bad boy, might become a bad man. There's the scar on her cheekbone I haven't asked about. I can't tell how young she was when she got it.

"That's ugly," she says. "This is ugly. What number was I?"

"Ten."

"I see," she says and stands there.

"You know, you're older than you think," she says. "When I saw your picture, the picture you sent me, the black and white, well, when I saw you, you're older than that picture."

"It's my book jacket photo. Whatever. You still went to bed with me."

"Ten in ten days. What were you trying to prove?"

"That I'm still the man. At least in my own eyes. That I'm still the man even if I can't get published."

"You are published. What were you trying to prove?"

"That I'm as young as my picture and all that means."

"You're not," she says.

"You're right. I'm not."

And if I'd met her when I was her age I might have cared, cared about her, cared about making our first moments together right there, cared about the way her eyes are suddenly the most beautiful kind of sad, the way she stands there, naked from the waist up, not shy about her body at all. I might have cared. But I'm not even sure that's true. I can't remember. I can't remember what I used to feel. I can't even remember what I felt when my first book was published and then my second, not really. I remember what I felt later. I remember it because I'm feeling it. I can't sell a book. I can't write a book. It's why I write stories now, and only now and then. I can make it through ten pages, fifteen pages, sometimes twenty. But I can't go longer than that. There's no adrenaline in me, nothing that pushes me forward to write the novel I could have written if everything I wrote had been published, if I'd been taken seriously the way serious writers are taken, if I were, and this is the word that keeps coming to me, significant. But I'm not. I'm insignificant. Insignificant is the word that's me.

Natalie puts on her bra.

"You don't have to wait around," she says. "You can leave if you want."

"Do you want me to leave?"

"I don't want anything."

The way she says it sounds the way I feel.

I walk to her. My T-shirt is still in my hand. I put it around the back of her neck and bring her head to me and kiss her for a long time.

"What was that for?" she says.

"That was for sounding so young and so old at the same time."

"That's you, isn't it?"

"More old than young. You made that clear."

I kiss her again. Mouth. Neck. Shoulder. I move her bra to the side, take her nipple in my mouth, move my tongue over it, slow and slow, make her nipple hard.

"I don't believe you," she says and puts her hands on my arms and moves me away. "The way you're kissing me. The way you put your shirt around my neck. It's rehearsed."

"My second book was optioned in Hollywood."

"I don't care. It's still rehearsed. I hope I never get that old."

I let my breath out slow.

For her. For me. Mostly for me. Not because I'm surprised. Not because I'm hurt. I'm not. Not really. Because it's what I do, punctuating the moment, emphasizing with an exhale, like emphasizing with a pause some small movement, a short line on the page.

"Take two," I say. "I hope you never get that old either."

"That sounds like a line too," she says. "I hope you write better than you play these tawdry scenes."

"Well done."

"Line," she says.

Ten. Tenure. If I didn't get the job when I got it, I wouldn't have gotten the job. Sometimes, at first when I thought I could really leave the city and teach somewhere else, then when I half-thought it, then when I knew I'd never leave my job, too far in, too settled, and so many bars in Manhattan, I'd send out my CV and cover letter. I just wanted to see, just wanted to know. The number was a non-number. Zero. I never got an offer. I never got an interview.

"Eleven," she says.

"You're already ten. You can't be eleven."

"Here's my bet. Make me feel like eleven, or at least less like ten. Make me feel outside your bet. I don't think you can. Bring some layers to it. Make it lyrical. Give me something to write about. Give me something more than a man who's feeling less than a man, who can't even make love without pretending."

"Make love. That's a fake term. Fucking is what it is."

"Even Hemingway didn't write the word *Fucking*. You're the fake. Make me feel outside your bet, or I'll write about you and it won't be lyrical. I'll mention your name and my whole class will look you up and see your two books and your author photo and read a few paragraphs of something you've written, and whatever they read will be tainted by my essay about how pitiful you seem. That's the best I can come up with right now. I'll be as mean as what you did to me and nine others."

Her eyes are steady. She doesn't look angry or hurt or sad. She looks tired, as tired as her raw voice sounds. I don't see anything fake in her eyes, anything pretend.

"Eleven," I say.

"If I feel you acting, I'll stop you. I'll push you off and tell you to leave. I'll start writing."

"You're right. My camera's always there. I'm aware of every-thing."

"That's on you. I don't know you. I know me and I know I'll start writing."

I don't use my shirt to bring her close. I don't put my hand on the back of her neck and bring her mouth to my mouth, a move I do. I don't stare at her, eyes to eyes, nod my head, another move. I just kiss her. I try to relax into the kiss. I keep my eyes closed. I feel her lips move away. I don't bring her back.

"Well," she says.

"Well," she says again like she's deciding something.

There's her. There's the wall behind her. There's the light more dark from the shades down.

There's still time before she needs to pick up her kid.

She stays where she is.

It's quiet here. Not rare for here. It's been quiet the whole time.

I move slowly.

Like she's new.

Like she's completely new.

Natalie takes me inside.

I move.

I just move.

I just move.

I just move.

These stories were first published in these litmags:

Black Belt	*Coe Review*
Half a Dead Man	*Hawaii Review*
Hollywood but not just Hollywood	*Tartts Eight*
Last Straws	*Cottonwood*
like forking toast at breakfast	*Fence*
My Painting of Me	*New Flash Fiction Review*
Practice Makes	*Pinyon Review*
Romance of the Seas	*the minnesota review*
ten	*The Rail*
The Aloha State	*Bryant Literary Review*

Versions of these stories were first published here:

A Picture of You	*Oxford Magazine*
Extra	*BODY*
Makeit	*riverSedge*

Acknowledgments:

Thank you to Joe Taylor and all at Livingston Press for selecting my story collection for the Tartt Fiction Award. I've valued Joe's guidance, and it's been easy, in the best sense, working with such a tightly-run university press. To Alec Shane, my agent, who has been editor and advocate over the years, a deep thank you. To my mom and dad, who started my writing life—our home that once was is still in me. To in-laws Kathleen Peratis, whose attention and care are a gift, and Tim Willert, whose kindness is steadfast, thank you. To Craig Gardner, my first NYC friend, I miss you. To Neil Bradley, who's read more of my work, pre-publication, than anyone, I value our adrenaline-fueled conversations that keep me pushing. To Jeffrey Heiman, colleague, co-editor of *J Journal,* and great friend, we talk words and sentences and scenes and all that's in between, and we're always laughing. And to Katherine, the woman I hoped for and found, and our beautiful son, Eben, you are my steady (and steadying) light. I love you both.

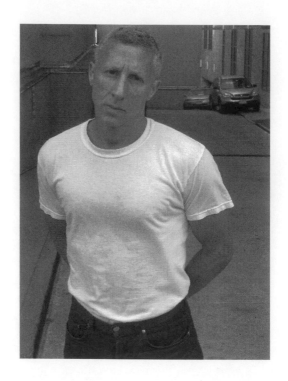

Adam Berlin has published four novels: *Headlock* (Algonquin Books), *Belmondo Style* (St. Martin's/The Publishing Triangle's Ferro-Grumley Award), *The Number of Missing* (Spuyten Duyvil), and *Both Members of the Club* (Texas Review Press/Clay Reynolds Prize). He teaches writing at John Jay College/CUNY in NYC and co-edits the litmag *J Journal*.